A Certain Magical Index

8

KAZUMA KAMACHI

ILLUSTRATION BY
KIYOTAKA HAIMURA

"Ahh, how careless of me!
My ribbon—it has gone into
the forbidden Big Sister zone!"

Academy City Tokiwadai Middle
School student **Kuroko Shirai**

"Weeell, after thinking about it more, maybe it didn't absolutely *need* to be you, Shirai…"

Officer of Judgment
Branch 177
Kazari Uiharu

"You made it
so far that I
would have
gladly been
your friend,
you know."

Academy City
Kirigaoka Girls'
Academy second-year
Awaki Musujime

"Bfpppft?! says Misaka says Misaka, toppling over at the sudden attack!"

Sisters, serial number 20001 **Last Order**

"Yeah, right. Here, I'll give you a shower to the face as thanks."

Academy City's strongest Level Five **Accelerator**

"Huh? Touma, I think someone is here. And at this hour, too."

Nun managing the Index of Prohibited Books **Index**

"I have a request, says Misaka, looking straight at you and speaking her mind."

Sisters, serial number 10032 **Little Misaka**

"Owwwwwwww!!"

Academy City High School student **Touma Kamijou**

contents

VOLUME 8

KAZUMA KAMACHI

ILLUSTRATION BY: KIYOTAKA HAIMURA

NEW YORK

A CERTAIN MAGICAL INDEX, Volume 8
KAZUMA KAMACHI

Translation by Andrew Prowse
Cover art by Kiyotaka Haimura

This book is a work of fiction. Names, characters, places, and incidents are the product of the author's imagination or are used fictitiously. Any resemblance to actual events, locales, or persons, living or dead, is coincidental.

TOARU MAJYUTSU NO INDEX
©KAZUMA KAMACHI 2006
All rights reserved.
Edited by ASCII MEDIA WORKS.
First published in Japan in 2006 by KADOKAWA CORPORATION, Tokyo.
English translation rights arranged with KADOKAWA CORPORATION, Tokyo,
through Tuttle-Mori Agency, Inc., Tokyo.

English translation © 2016 by Yen Press, LLC

Yen On
1290 Avenue of the Americas
New York, NY 10104

Visit us at yenpress.com
facebook.com/yenpress
twitter.com/yenpress
yenpress.tumblr.com

First Yen On Edition: August 2016

Yen On is an imprint of Yen Press, LLC.
The Yen On name and logo are trademarks of Yen Press, LLC.

The publisher is not responsible for websites (or their content) that are not owned by the publisher.

Library of Congress Cataloging-in-Publication Data

Names: Kamachi, Kazuma, author. | Haimura, Kiyotaka, 1973- illustrator. |
Prowse, Andrew (Andrew R.), translator. | Hinton, Yoshito, translator.
Title: A certain magical index / Kazuma Kamachi ; illustration by Kiyotaka Haimura.
Other titles: To aru majyutsu no kinsho mokuroku. (Light novel). English
Description: First Yen On edition. | New York : Yen On, 2014-
Identifiers: LCCN 2014031047 (print) | LCCN 2016021552 (ebook) | ISBN
 9780316339124 (v. 1 : pbk.) | ISBN 9780316259422 (v. 2 : pbk.) | ISBN
 9780316340540 (v. 3 : pbk.) | ISBN 9780316340564 (v. 4 : pbk.) | ISBN
 9780316340595 (v. 5 : pbk.) | ISBN 9780316340601 (v. 6 : pbk.) | ISBN
 9780316316576 (v. 1 : ebook) | ISBN 9780316316583 (v. 2 : ebook) | ISBN
 9780316316606 (v. 3 : ebook) | ISBN 9780316316613 (v. 4 : ebook) | ISBN
 9780316316637 (v. 5 : ebook) | ISBN 9780316316644 (v. 6 : ebook)
Subjects: | CYAC: Magic—Fiction. | Ability—Fiction. | Nuns—Fiction. |
Japan—Fiction. | Science fiction. | BISAC: FICTION / Fantasy / General. |
FICTION / Science Fiction / Adventure.
Classification: LCC PZ7.1.K215 Ce 2014 (print) | LCC PZ7.1.K215 (ebook) | DDC [Fic]—dc23
LC record available at https://lccn.loc.gov/2014031047

ISBNs: 978-0-316-35992-4 (paperback)
 978-0-316-35995-5 (ebook)

10 9 8 7 6 5 4 3 2 1

RRD-C

Printed in the United States of America

PROLOGUE

Counted on One Hand
A_Tokiwa-Dai's_World.

Tokiwadai Middle School.

Not only was it said to be one of the top five elite schools in Academy City, an organization for supernatural ability development that boasted a size one-third of Tokyo's, it was also a world leader in schools for young ladies. Its entrance requirements were incredibly strict—one anecdote suggested it had flat-out rejected a member of a certain country's nobility, nearly developing into an international incident.

Its school grounds were shared with four other young ladies' schools adjacent to it. This was not done out of a lack of available space but rather so they could all contribute to expenditures and also to create a tight security system.

This was the Garden of Learning, a communal zone fifteen times the size of a normal school. But despite being so much larger than other schools, it didn't seem that big. There were more than a few building extensions made for experimentation and use in specialized curricula. Plus, every piece of equipment for ability development they used was produced within the Garden of Learning—they outsourced absolutely nothing, just to keep their original technology from getting out. There were a lot of manufacturing facilities and stores, too, as a result. All these facilities—from the outside, at least—were unified in their western style. The campus seemed like an entire small town on the Mediterranean had been picked up and planted here.

The Garden of Learning was so distinct inside that even the design of signposts and traffic lights was unlike those outside.

"Roads paved in stone, buildings made of marble...The very height of inefficiency!"

The date was September 14. The afternoon broiled with the lingering summertime heat as in the middle of the schoolyard, a girl with pigtails who looked like a track-and-field athlete in her tank top and shorts spoke to herself as she looked at the school building in the distance. She was Kuroko Shirai, and she sounded worn down by the heat.

The schoolyard was paved in stone, bringing to mind the open space in front of the British Museum. However, if an expert surveyor were to measure its surface, he or she wouldn't find a single uneven centimeter or the least bit of sloping. It wasn't mere stone that they'd used, either. The naked eye couldn't tell the difference, but examination with an electron microscope would reveal that it was a special building material produced in Academy City.

The glittering schoolyard hadn't even a speck of dirt—not so much a grain of the white powder schools always used for drawing track lines for physical education classes. At the moment, Shirai was in class, currently in the middle of an ability-measuring competition. The lines for *that* had been drawn using something else. They were made of light. Thousands upon thousands of fibers of light were hung vertically in every nook and cranny of the schoolyard. They emitted light, which gathered together and freely "drew" light rays like some electronic billboard.

Currently, the beams were forming a small ring around Shirai with a giant fan shape extending from it. It looked quite similar to the circle athletes stood in for shot put events, but *her* fan was far narrower in angle than that.

And lined up next to Shirai, with the exact same shapes, were more girls wearing gym outfits inside those circles. It was set up like a batting cage.

Shirai had the ability to teleport. In simple terms, it allowed her to ignore three-dimensional space and instantly warp anything at hand, including herself, to a distant location. Its only restriction was that the object needed to be in contact with her skin.

The Level of teleportation users depended heavily on three conditions: the size (mass) of the object, the maximum range it could be teleported, and its accuracy. This shot put–like business was a method of measuring that. Unlike normal shot put, however, she would launch hers as far as possible but also drop it at a precise location.

Incidentally, Shirai was the only teleporter at Tokiwadai Middle School. The girls around her were all actually espers with abilities involving throwing weapons.

Plop. Shirai could see far off in the distance something falling.

She had just teleported a sandbag weighing 120 kilograms.

A few moments later, the ground by her feet started displaying new characters made of light.

Result: 78m 23cm / 54 cm away from indicated position / Overall evaluation: 5

As she saw those numbers, she sighed, her pigtails swinging left to right. "Jeez, I am in spectacularly terrible condition…I may even forget how to speak Japanese correctly. I'm so bad at warping big, heavy things far away! If we were talking fifty meters or so, I could have landed it within millimeters."

In the first place, the limit to her warp distance was 81.5 meters, and at most she could warp a 130.7-kilogram object. The warp distance and weight of the object weren't correlated to her ability—even with a lighter object, she couldn't send it any farther. On the other hand, the closer she aimed to her distance limit, the less precise she got.

To add to that, her mental state greatly affected her ability values. With this heat, it was only natural she'd have less precision if they told her to go to her limit right away.

But I can't make excuses like that, or I'll never be Level Five, she thought in self-deprecation, breathing a heavy sigh. Suddenly, there was a guffaw from the shot put throwing circle next to her.

"Hee-hee-hee. Oh, Miss Shirai, if you get so obviously happy or sad at some numbers a machine is shooting at you, it only shows your caliber to those around you, yes? If you do not find a firmer basis of judgment within yourself...Pfft!"

Shirai, exasperated, turned to her side.

That hair, so unnecessarily silky and smooth that it looked more unnatural than attractive. That folding fan in her right hand, despite the fact she was wearing the same gym uniform with tank top and shorts as Shirai. That smile she was hiding with the extravagant fan at her lips. The girl was one year older than her (electives had students from every grade), and her name was Mitsuko Konkou.

Konkou was a Level Four aerohand. She specialized in creating points of wind propulsion on objects and firing them like missiles—a crazy rocket girl.

"...You revealed how petty you are when you started laughing uncontrollably at someone who was feeling down," Shirai responded, turning a cheek in irritation.

"Oh, my. You do say some silly things, Miss Fifty-four Centimeters Off. By the way, Miss Shirai, in my humble opinion, your abilities have been rather dull as of late, haven't they? And that... Oh, my, are you ignoring me? Miss Shirai, I will send a favorable wind your way, so by all means, take a look, won't you?"

Konkou flapped her folding fan at Shirai, who looked at it resentfully.

Pleased, Konkou continued, rapidly waving her fan with its sickly sweet fragrance. "Back to what I was saying—the dulling of your abilities is because you are trying to process parts of space you don't need to, is it not? You should simply tighten your calculations more, yes?"

"...Don't butt in on my business. Besides, you don't fundamentally think about eleven dimensions the same way as the first three!"

"No, no, I haven't butted into your business just yet. You see, I was considering creating a faction soon. I would gladly welcome you into it if you had free time, or even if you would force yourself to clear your schedule. What do you think? Consider it like a study group, won't you? Perhaps we will gain new perspectives on how we do our mental calculations by learning how other espers control their abilities."

Shirai sighed and frowned.

A faction.

A very stiff, formal word—for what was essentially a hangout group.

This, however, was Tokiwadai Middle School. Its mission statement was to raise people who would be useful to the world by the end of their compulsory education. From the moment a student enrolled, she was subject to every kind of research field imaginable. Many of their names would go down in history.

Factions were gatherings of like-minded students who borrowed the school's facilities and raised money all to immortalize their names in the minds of the entire country...In that way, they were much like clubs. The larger factions could secure connections both personal and financial as well as proprietary knowledge. Most students at the forefront of these groups borrowed from that power to achieve meritorious deeds.

Certain students could do these things alone without needing to join a faction, but from financial and logistical perspectives, it was easier to join a club and use their paperwork to request those things from the school. The more members and achievements a faction had, the more it would ascend within the school—they were no different from normal clubs in that respect.

That was why large factions had significant power both within Tokiwadai Middle School and outside it. Just being part of a large faction was a form of honor, and the renown gained for being the one to create it was nothing to shake a stick at.

And these young ladies had powers easily superior to handguns and pistols and connections to all sorts of different spheres—when they formed their little groups, their factions had a much more direct, clear sort of *power*. Powers, some of which were dangerous even used alone and for one's personal gain, could be used in concert with others to inflict massive damage to surrounding areas.

Thus, she said this: "It would be easier for you if you gave it up. If you made a faction, it would get destroyed in two seconds."

"Wha…?"

"You don't understand? If you were strong enough to create a dangerous faction, another one would have crushed you already. Obviously this is news to you, so perhaps you should get a grip on how much less powerful you are than them."

"Th-that is not true!" protested Konkou, indignant, her face turning red. "W-with my own abilities and my Konkou pedigree, I would destroy any faction in a fair fight, no matter how strong it was—" Before she finished, though, her face went white.

Whump!!

A sudden explosive tremor hit them—and not only the school building, or only the gymnasium, or only the schoolyard. Every object on the entire school grounds creaked, squealed, and bounced around.

There was a pool behind the school building, though it wasn't visible from here because it was on the other side. That's where the explosion originated.

And despite an entire building standing between them, a thin spray of water hit Konkou's flushed cheeks, immediately giving her cause to shudder. *Something* had made that blast of pool water fly all the way out here, after all.

"…Wh…What in the world was that?" Konkou, surprised, the droplets of water striking her face, was shivering as though she'd just been licked. Then she put her hand to her cheek, stared up at the sky, then back down to the school building.

"Oh, that's right. You only transferred in for the second semester, so you don't know. That was the Tokiwadai Middle School's ace."

That made Konkou remember.

There could only be one girl standing there at the pool behind the school building.

A girl who, despite being a ranged attack user like Shirai and Konkou, was an esper so tremendously strong that it put the teachers at Tokiwadai to shame for being unable to measure her enormous destructive power with their usual instruments.

The school had assigned her a curriculum particular to her needs. Even all the water stored in the entire pool wasn't enough to dull her power—she could destroy the entire school building along with all the measuring equipment. A Level Five, a Superpower, of which only two existed in all of Tokiwadai Middle School.

Mikoto Misaka—the Railgun.

She was beholden to no faction and gave favorable treatment to no one.

The visage of the "older sister" she idolized came to Kuroko Shirai's mind, but she shook it off, instead asking in an exasperated tone, "Miss Konkou, do you really have the resolve to face such an absurd attack head-on?"

An innocent question. Mitsuko Konkou's face went blue, unable to respond.

"It may be true that you would have great influence in Tokiwa-dai Middle School if you created a faction and became its leader. But if you only want to make one so that you can act arrogant and insolent, Big Sister will come right away and put a stop to it."

Another explosion ripped through the air as if in response.

CHAPTER 1

Girls After School
After_School_of_Angels.

1

"And that's what happened, Big Sister."

Tokiwadai Middle School had three shower rooms.

In one of them, called the Returners' Bath—the one attached to the school building mainly for girls to get their appearances in order before leaving school—was Kuroko Shirai, covered in white steam and water that was the perfect warmth. The drops running down her delicate body pushed the soap bubbles clinging to her chest down toward her stomach.

"Oh, wow, the water spray made it that far, huh?" replied Mikoto from across the partition as though the whole thing was absurd. "You know, they were making such a big deal out of it, but it doesn't feel like I did much. I was still so wrapped up in controlling my own strength! Such a small pool would never do anything to stop a *real* attack."

The shower room was the size of five classrooms put together, and there were white partitions and swinging doors installed around each of the close to ninety shower faucets here. The partitions were one thing, but the doors were made of frosted glass and were only large enough to cover the thighs to the chest of the middle school student of average height. They weren't made for really tall girls, and sometimes they would talk about needing to hunch over a bit, lest they expose themselves.

"Besides, even if I needed to stop someone, I'd try to resolve the situation with talking. If it were as small a problem as that swimming pool was, anyway. I do try to at least have the good sense to choose my attacks based on my opponent, though. I mean, the only one I'm comfortable shooting something full power at is that idiot."

The last bit made it sound like she was reassured by the fact, which caused Shirai's eyebrow to twitch. As the sensation of the lukewarm water hitting the white bubbles on her stomach and making them slowly creep down to her thighs hit, she thought, *That idiot. She's talking about that idiot again...*

Shirai, with only one of her eyebrows twitching, reached above the swinging door. There were two thin ribbons for tying her hair into twin tails there.

She suddenly and deliberately dropped one of them on the floor. There was a pool of warm shower water on the white marble, so when the ribbon fell into it, the thin film of running water carried it toward the nearby shower area through the gap in the partition.

"Ahh, how careless of me! My ribbon—it has gone into the forbidden Big Sister zone!"

"Yes, don't you dare come *accidentally* teleporting into here!"

Right before she was about to teleport, Mikoto yelled, then Shirai heard a loud bang on the partition from the other side. The students in the other shower areas paused for a moment out of surprise.

With her timing thrown completely off due to the sound and the impact, Shirai was forced to cancel her teleportation. In order for her to trigger her ability, she needed to substitute theoretical values of eleven dimensions into this three-dimensional world she was bound to, then re-form her grasp on reality. The calculations involved were extremely cumbersome, and sudden panic or surprise could render her power useless.

"Heh-heh. Such a precise interception, and with no planning involved. This is proof of the natural compatibility that exists between our bodies—even our breathing matches. Heh. Heh-heh-heh-heh!!"

"You're being gross, so I don't want to respond to that. Anyway, take your ribbon."

Mikoto's slender, wet hand suddenly poked over the top of the partition. Entwined in her fingers was the soaked ribbon. Shirai thanked her and took the ribbon. The thin cloth was a little warm.

Shirai slowly ran her fingers from the top of her body down, getting the more persistent bubbles off, then twisted the shower faucet to stop the water. "By the way, Big Sister, would you happen to have plans after school today?" She turned back to the partition next to her and got a few drops of warm water off her chest that had floated down from her collarbone.

"Yeah. I'm going to take a nap, just like I do every other day of the year," answered Mikoto crudely. Shirai heard a rummaging noise—maybe she was fishing around for the little shampoo bottle in her carry-on shower kit.

"If only that were true—I would have full access to you while you were sleeping, too..."

"Don't sigh like that. It makes it sound like you're *actually* disappointed. It gives me the creeps. Anyway, did you need something from me after school?"

Shirai heard the sound of scrubbing bubbles. The scent of a sweet shampoo wafted to her nose. The sound of the water past the partition grew louder; she must have turned up how much was coming out of the showerhead.

"No, I didn't need anything in particular." Shirai leaned her back against the partition. "But, well, once in a while! Once in a while, I was just thinking we could go shopping together or eat some cake or something. I have been so busy with Judgment that we haven't had much chance to go out together lately. Frankly speaking, I, Kuroko, have been feeling a bit lonely as of late. And besides, you mentioned that for the last few days you have been searching for a certain accessory, no?"

"Kuroko…" Mikoto's tone over the partition changed into something more sympathetic. *G-gallant! Kuroko, you will be gallant and brave today! She might deny it, but she wants nothing more than to embrace me in her loving, dependable arms and fawn over me. Hu-hu, eheh-he-heh-ah-hah!!* Kuroko Shirai grinned like a bandit—it was a good thing the partition was here so Mikoto couldn't see it.

Utterly ignorant of her expression, Mikoto started speaking gently to her underclassman. "You know, every day after your Judgment job after school, you stuff your face with a lot of candy, don't you? That's why no matter how hard you try to diet, your belly never goes back in, isn't it?"

A moment later…

Bandit's smile still on her face, Kuroko Shirai teleported to Mikoto Misaka and attacked.

More precisely, she moved to a position diagonally above Mikoto.

There are times when a woman must do a dropkick even when she knows she's already lost.

2

The Garden of Learning, the shared area created for five schools for young ladies, was an extremely small town.

Shirai thought of it like a U.S. military base in Japan, though that particular analogy was questionable. Large fences kept out-

siders from coming in, and there were both residential areas and laboratories on the premises. In fact, it even included essential commercial outlets like cafés and clothing shops. The town was packed, but only with necessities.

Shirai and Mikoto walked through it.

The area was supposed to be fenced off, but there were buses driven by women inside it. The students here each had one of five different uniforms, and all were girls. In a way, this Garden of Learning, which could be called a strange sight, looked like an old town on the sea with lots of buildings of white and roads paved with stone. The buildings were close in design to western-style houses, but many had squarish silhouettes that looked like the traditional triangular Japanese roof had been squished down flat. It was a shape used in places with not much rain. It also looked like modern buildings had been remixed using older decorations.

But for such a town implanted from the western hemisphere, there were two things missing.

One was a church.

And the other was a statue of a person.

The reason for the first went without saying, and the latter was usually a religious figure or saint anyway.

The town may have been styled after western towns, but without those two things, it wasn't built to the same specifications—normally in real western towns, the houses spread out from religious facilities and plazas.

Instead, the schools took on the role. From overhead, the five of them were easy to see. They were bunched up and linked by slender paths around them, giving the appearance of a spiderweb, an intricate pattern of intertwining roads with countless intersections.

Because of that, the paths in the Garden of Learning weren't very wide. The area had already been limited, but they'd been adding to experimental facilities one after another for a long time, making the narrow roads weave among buildings like a labyrinth.

Anyway.

After school, in some weird town, there were two girls walking shoulder to shoulder.

Kuroko Shirai and Mikoto Misaka.

They were young ladies of Tokiwadai Middle School, the object of adoration for all girls in Academy City, but for some reason, both their hair was ruffled and messy—the harmful side effect of their brawl.

Mikoto, slumping tiredly, ran a hand through her hair to fix it. "…You know, you can't just dropkick someone in the face fully naked! You were so open and unguarded that I froze up instead. Seriously."

"Hee-hee. I've begun to understand you recently, Big Sister. It may be absurd to challenge a superpowered electromaster to a fair fight, but there's a lot of moisture in the shower room, so you can't use your electric attacks because they might cause short circuits! But my greatest miscalculation was not realizing you knew how to fight dirty with your bare hands!" Shirai ended with a regretful tone and grinned drily. Neither looked anything like someone raised under Tokiwadai's founding principle: to produce people who could function in the real world even during their compulsory education.

Shirai swung her flimsy bag from side to side and continued smiling defiantly. Mikoto turned an eye to her and said, "But you really were serious about dieting, huh?"

"I was wondering more how you have such a perfect figure despite not thinking about it. Hah! You have some trick, don't you? Where you control your bioelectric field and efficiently burn off the fat, a kind of trick only you would have…?!"

"I don't have anything like that, so stop looking at me like I'm some kind of god. I said, I don't have a trick! Don't grab my shoulders and shake me so hard! It's not like I don't understand how you feel, but doesn't our school prohibit that kind of thing?"

Unreasonable diets obstructed growth, which presented a danger for ability development, so some schools banned their students from doing them. Shirai stopped swinging around her bag, sighed, and replied, "Abilities are important, too, but worth throwing away your femininity for? I don't want to turn into some enormous human teleportation device."

"But I heard once you start a diet, the first thing you lose is fat from your chest. Also, if you overdo it, the oils that make your skin shiny get all dry, and it's easier for your hair to fall out because it's not getting enough nutrition."

"Ahhhh! I don't want to hear this kind of terrible trivia!" shouted Shirai, covering her ears and shaking her head.

Normally such a conversation would be seen as eccentric behavior in Academy City, but the other female students who overheard them certainly sympathized, so they got no odd looks. There was even one girl nearby with a French fry in her fingers who gave a pained smile before returning the snack to its container.

Shirai didn't think Mikoto would broach the subject of weight or makeup in the city normally, either. For one reason or another, she'd worry about men staring at her. From that perspective, the Garden of Learning was still a girls' school according to her mind.

They walked through the artificially western town.

There were no big stores like department stores or malls in the Garden of Learning. Shops that dealt solely in one necessity for each thing they needed for the curriculum or school life, like gym uniforms or stationery, were on the rise, so the town was stuffed with little shops that specialized in just one item. The exceptionally giant buildings were all research institutions.

Every one of the labyrinthine paths and lanes had turned into shopping districts.

Shirai spotted a certain signboard among them, then took Mikoto's hand and pulled her into the shop.

After she entered, she sighed, disappointed. "When you said you needed to go somewhere, you meant *here*?"

"Oh, my, but this is essential to living!" answered Shirai, as though it were totally obvious.

It was a lingerie shop.

The snug, compact store featured an interior design that used mainly darkly colored materials, in the same vein as antique stores and souvenir shops. Both the orange evening glow streaming through the windows and the light bulbs adorned with lamp decorations filled the interior with a soft light. On the whole, it had clearly been done this way to create a relaxing space.

But decorating the place was women's underwear of all tints and hues. Their laces and bright coloring didn't quite meld with the idea of a relaxed shopping atmosphere. Instead, perhaps they made the goods stand out more to give them a stronger impression in the minds of their customers.

"Well, I mean, I kind of feel like you shouldn't come here with people you know. It just seems like you're flaunting your taste in underwear."

"There's no need to be shy. Such concerns mean nothing between the two of us. I am already well aware that Big Sister leans toward the pastel-colored, childish underwear—*Ow, oww!* Please do not grab my ear so suddenly, Big Sister!"

"...Teleportation really is a huge pain in the butt, isn't it, Kuroko? Come on, cough it up. When do you check what underwear I'm wearing every day?!"

"Wh-why does it matter so much? You see my underwear every single day, too, do you not?"

"Not because I want to! You really shouldn't wear a sheer negligee as pajamas! I mean, you're probably showing it off on purpose because it makes you happy or something, but still!"

"Oh, if we are talking about pajamas, then your tendency toward baggy, pastel-colored, childish ones is rather—*Ow!* I know quite well that you have been all about the queen look this year—*Ow, ack?!*"

Mikoto was pulling on Shirai's right ear, but she looked happy about it.

Despite all the commotion, they weren't drawing stares from those around them. The other guests amounted to a group of three girls from another young ladies' school, and behind the counter there was one old lady, both the proprietress and a lace craftsman, who looked like she'd come as a set with the counter and had been sitting there for decades. None seemed to mind their noise—the proprietress was even reading an English-language newspaper. Their sharp squeaking wasn't loud enough for people to think of them as a disturbance in this girl-filled Garden of Learning.

"Oh, Big Sister. Do you not think the two-piece set on display over there would suit you perfectly?"

"I'm pulling on your ear, here. How are you making such calm recommendations?…Hey, what?! You can see through eighty percent of that lace underwear. You'd only choose something like that to make people laugh!"

"This store does specialize in underwear, however, so would it not be more natural for them to stock professional underwear rather than unprofessional underwear?"

"…You make it sound like you're an expert on the topic, Kuroko."

"I, of course, specialize in many things that have the potential to bring the color of embarrassment to your cheeks, Big Si—*Ow!!* …Y-you mustn't keep doing this. This sort of relationship is starting to be rather *thrilling*. Fu...fu-fu. I suppose having Big Sister grab part of my body in broad daylight and making me moan is a perfectly valid form of entertainment!"

"Kuroko? If I pull your ear any more, it'll tear off and we'll make a mess."

Mikoto smiled and stretched Shirai's ear out, but she hadn't overlooked one thing. When Mikoto had glanced at the two-piece lace set she'd recommended to her, she'd blushed and hurried to peel her eyes from it. Shirai grinned, very much happy at having seen Mikoto's profile filled with embarrassment, but she suddenly had a thought and noticed Mikoto had, at some point, begun looking at something else with a serious look on her face.

"?"

Shirai, vaguely interested, looked in the same direction.

The world outside the windows facing the street was covered in the glow of the afternoon sun, and a blimp was floating by, far away in the sky. It stood out as strange given the old-fashioned, western-style town below. A big screen was attached to its side, displaying today's news in Academy City.

The headline they could see from there was about the successful launch of a space shuttle in the United States. The VTR of the shuttle launch taken with cameras from multiple angles was being played over and over and over again.

Mikoto stared at the news seriously for a long time, forgetting all about underwear, but Shirai wasn't interested. "There's been a lot of them lately. If I recall, France, Russia, and Spain all did launches last week. And aren't China and Pakistan scheduled to launch later this month? My type-three economics teacher always goes off on tangents about the advantages and disadvantages of space enterprises."

As she spoke, she gently prodded one of Mikoto's earlobes with her fingertip.

"Bwah! Wh-what was that for, Kuroko?!" She quickly turned back to Shirai. "W-well, Academy City launched one last month, too. Wait, you're taking another useless elective, aren't you? Also, don't poke me in the earlobes! And no, it's going to make me *more* angry if you try and tickle them!!"

Tokiwadai Middle School was an organization for the special education of gifted children who could become leaders in every field the world had to offer during their compulsory education. That meant their classes were put together differently than normal middle school textbooks.

"Apparently, a long time ago...the technology and funds needed to launch multistage rockets and space shuttles using large launch sites meant not just any country or organization could do so. But now things are different, I think...I have a report due on it this weekend, so I've been researching it...," she said, casually suggesting a black lace two-piece to Mikoto.

"I don't think you'll ever have to use type-three economics, though. Well, I guess if you have a report on it, I'll tell you. When we got the technology to strap a rocket to the bottom of an airplane and launch it from midair, it brought the barrier to the entryway down. They developed it at the beginning of the century, so it won't be in any of the older reference materials. Be careful of that when you're finding sources for your report." She sighed, shoving the black lace underwear back at Shirai without changing her expression.

Then, she noted a particular pair of light yellow panties and seemed to be interested, but..."Oh, Big Sister. If you really insist on being *that* childish, everyone is going to lose interest in you."

Mikoto stared at her with eyes asking, *What?* but this was something Shirai wasn't going to budge on. Perhaps sensing something from Shirai's stiff expression, Mikoto reluctantly turned to other underwear. But to her, the action was precisely what she figured a child would do.

She sighed. "Still, with the entire body of knowledge on the subject changing like that, it gets really muddled up. I seem to have my work cut out for me. I cannot just discard the older reference materials, either, because they may have information newer ones do not."

"Learning how to tell old information from new and incorrect from correct is what it means to study it! Besides, the space industry is prone to change—if you talk like that, it'll be a pain for you to memorize things. Like how the industry was energized by privatization, or how new records get set all the time and they have to keep rewriting the time line—*Pfft!* W-wait, Kuroko! That may not be childish, but it's going way too far…!!" spurted Mikoto despite herself when she saw the completely exposed—to the point of bad taste—underwear Shirai had picked up.

"??? What's the matter, Big Sister?"

"N-no, nothing, I don't care. Everyone has his or her own taste in underwear. Just make sure the R.A.s or the counselors don't catch wind of that." Mikoto looked away from the insane underwear Shirai was holding and took a deep breath. "W-well, it's a tough subject. Places that already had their own launch sites don't want to let newcomers break into the space R&D marketplace. Places with the new technology want to show they have things cheaper and more reliable than the old rockets and shuttles. If old tech or new tech is supported, then the other will go on the decline. So everyone's just doing a ton of launches and trying to prove to their sponsors that their own tech is more trustworthy." Mikoto still kept her eyes from the underwear in Shirai's hands, but she did glance over from time to time. She tried to keep it in but still ended up accidentally muttering, "Why not just be naked at that point…?"

"??? Why do you keep looking away from things like this?" she asked, tilting her head, a few different pairs of underwear she liked in her arms. "Academy City is the one place that has both kinds of technology, so there would be no problems there. Plus we're monopolizing all the deals with our biggest sponsor, the Japanese government, so it's pretty comfortable, but—*Ack.*"

She stopped, bringing her hand to her mouth. She felt her lips split a little.

Mikoto watched her and asked, "Why not put on some lip balm? Air conditioning dries you out pretty badly."

"Th-that is all right. In fact, I've been fresh out of it since yesterday."

Makeup in general was prohibited at Tokiwadai Middle School. The regulations were recklessly strict, too—obvious lipstick and mascara went without saying, but even practical, medicinal lip balm and hand cream (which everyone doubted even fell into the category of "makeup") would be targeted by the rule.

Therefore, it had become tradition among the girls to use just little enough of it so that normal people wouldn't be able to tell the difference. One might notice it if they got up close, but the color and gloss of Mikoto's and Shirai's lips were very slightly different. Though it had originally been a compromise out of necessity, this style was steadily becoming a little popular even outside Tokiwadai, along with the mysterious words of "ladylike manners."

"Hmm..." Mikoto fished through her bag and came out with a stick of medicinal lip balm. "Then let's drop by the cosmetics shop after this and get some things. You can use this in the meantime if you want."

"?!" Kuroko Shirai gave a start when she looked at the lip balm, devoid of any sexiness, that was being nonchalantly held out for her.

Her eyes opened wide and she began to tremble all over. *L-lip balm. Big, Big Sister's...Big Sister's, her, her lips, they've been on it every day, it's been on her beautiful lips, this lip balm!! Ah, ah. Kuroko, yes, Kuroko, yeaaaaaaaaaaaahhhhhhhhhh!!*

"Huh? What? H-hey, why did you make the whole thing come out—Hey, wait, wait, stop, stop, Kuroko! Why the heck are you trying to eat the stupid thing?!"

"Hah!!…I-I am so suddenly surprised and stunned at this that I think I may accidentally devour the entire thing."

"I have a good guess as to *why*, but that is a new one. It was in a three-pack. Besides, normally people don't want to use lip balm other people have used."

"Eh…A new one?" She clicked her tongue. "…What a disappointment. Ah, however! Then if I give the lip balm I used back to Big Sister, then…!"

"I don't need it back. I have two others anyway, so you can have it. Hey, stop that! Don't try to put lip balm you just used on my lips by force!"

Shirai and Mikoto began to fight like main characters of a Hollywood movie where one grabs a handgun and they start to wrestle. Suddenly, though, Mikoto stopped dead.

That's when Shirai realized it—Mikoto wasn't looking at her. Her eyes had been stolen by something else, something behind her.

"?" Dubious, she turned around to look.

They were breast pads.

Mainly worn underneath underwear by girls without confidence in their own chest, said to preserve their pride and dignity—yes, *those* breast pads. In actuality, however, in the Garden of Learning, populated only by girls—in other words, with no one to be prideful toward—they were not particularly in demand; they were leftover products sitting in the corner, their sorrow floating around them.

A bit confused, Shirai cocked her head just a little…and then remembered.

Mikoto had said something while they were walking through town, hadn't she?

But I heard once you start a diet, the first thing you lose is fat from your chest.

"Ha-ha, so it was bothering you! Oh, Big Sister, *pfft.* I suppose you have weighed your bust and waist on a scale and chosen the former, yes?"

"Wha...?" Mikoto stiffened.

"No...That is not it. You would not have such attachment to your breast growth, Big Sister. Which means you probably harbor slightly ambiguous hopes, such as wanting to have an adult body quickly or wanting people to stop treating you like a child. Ahh, how praiseworthy you are, Big Sister! Who could possibly be the lucky gentleman you want to go that far to present yourself to? Could the one in your heart really be an older man? Come to think of it, you seemed to be waiting for someone in front of the dormitory on the last day of summer vacation. He certainly did not appear to be a middle school student, did he?"

A provocation with this sort of timing? Shirai thought for sure she'd earn a punch from the girl. And she already had the entire conversation after the punch planned out in her head.

However...

Mikoto Misaka was a Level Five esper in Academy City, even called the ace of Tokiwadai Middle School. And instead, her face went red, and she looked down, not saying a word.

"Oh? Big Sister? Hey, Big Sister—"

Then Kuroko Shirai's face went pale. *I-I meant it as a joke, but she's taking it so seriously! Is she really, seriously, truly...Him?! That gentleman?!—huh. That freaking monkeeeeeeeeeey!!*

The face of a certain youth came to her mind and she bit into her handkerchief. Actually, she was practically tearing the thing apart. In her brain, she ripped the handkerchief to pieces. It took some time for her to calm down. When she finally did, she saw Mikoto looking at the breast pads in their vinyl packaging out of the corner of her eye, pretending not to be interested at all. She muttered something along the lines of, "H-huh, so some people do seriously use those things," working very hard to keep the interest from her face but still obviously extremely interested.

"...Breast pads come in all varieties. Whoa, like this one—it's like water balloons, or it has gel inside or something."

Mikoto's engrossment got Shirai angry, but she would never ignore something her beloved big sister said. Feeling gloomy about a number of things now, she sighed. "Apparently they stuff vinyl bags with gel in them when you get breast implants, too. I mean, most people would need some sort of device to have them swaying all over the place."

"Swaying all over the place...Th-they have a lot of different shapes, too."

"Everyone has their own needs, I suppose. Oh, Big Sister, I think yours would become that type after your modest chest grows some more, do you not?"

"Don't point to it! There are other customers in here!!"

Mikoto hastily pushed Shirai's finger away, but she kept her eyes and attention on the product Shirai had pointed out. Shirai, looking distant, sighed—if she shoved such a gigantic breast pad into her bra, everyone would clearly notice.

For a few moments, Mikoto forgot about the time, single-mindedly observing the breast pads. Then, suddenly, she took a step back from the shelf they were on and tilted her head. "But in the end, as soon as you took your clothes off, the truth would come out."

"...?! B-Big Sister. D-do not tell me that you have already planned so far into the future?!"

"Eh? Uh, oh! No, that's not it, Kuroko!! Gym class! I'm talking about changing during gym class!!" Mikoto insisted, shaking her head in a fluster. Shirai's face remained comically locked in an expression of surprise.

3

Academy City bathed in the evening glow.

The Garden of Learning used white as its standard color for buildings. They were extremely good at reflecting the color of the sky. The traffic flow of the young ladies, separated into five different school uniforms, was gathering at the terminal—the time of the last bus was approaching. Like Mikoto and Shirai, their dorms were probably outside of the Garden of Learning.

They weren't required to use the bus, but some of these young ladies were ignorant of the ways of the world, scared even of Academy City, from which they were isolated. Some even lived in a mental bubble containing only their dormitory, the bus, and the Garden of Learning.

Shirai and Mikoto walked leisurely through the frantic going-home rush. Actually, it was more like they were exhausted and unable to join the rush. The flimsy bags in their hands swayed to and fro without energy.

"I-I told you a hundred times, I'm only talking about when I get changed for gym. I-I mean, th-th-there's no guy I'm into or not into—you know what, it doesn't matter at all anyway."

"A-and as I've said a thousand times, it is certainly too early for you to plan for a future that involves taking off your clothes in front of a gentleman, yes?"

"Argh! You're so bad at listening, you bad-taste full-exposure lace-underwear buyer!"

"B-bad taste?! Th-that underwear *you* found was so cutesy it was just childish instead, and as a fellow girl, it creeps me out!"

They began struggling with each other again. They didn't last long, though, since their protracted argument earlier had drained their stamina. They both sighed and fell limp again.

They didn't use the bus to begin with, so they didn't mind when the last bus came. With the passing of the students on their way home, stores were already beginning to close up. Shirai glanced at the cozy shops as she went by. "Big Sister, I will without a doubt make further inquiries into the truth of this matter at a later time. But what shall we do now? A good amount of time has passed because of our arguing. My current Kuroko Plan was to go for a light meal after shopping."

"I see. I'll certainly clear up the misunderstanding later, then. Shouldn't we call it quits for today? Everything in the Garden of Learning closes up early."

"Hmmmm. There are plenty of shops outside, though. Things only just begin when we leave. We could go for a dessert course at the Kuromitsu House."

"Umm, Kuroko, it's because you give in to these temptations that you'll end up being happy and plump in places you don't want—*Eek?!*"

Before Mikoto could finish, she sensed a menacing outburst. Next to her, Shirai's face was down, so she couldn't see her expression well. She was muttering to herself.

"K-Kuroko? I promise, I was about to wrap that up by saying if you eat that stuff, you'd really just need to exercise a little!"

"Big Sister...If you continue to say things that wound a maiden's heart like that, I will gladly teleport your clothing away in a busy street in broad daylight."

Shirai, her hands out and fingers wiggling, was the natural enemy of girls everywhere. If she touched anything with those hands, whether it was a skirt or underwear, it'd be warped to wherever she liked. Half-naked or fully nude—everything was completely in her control.

As Mikoto feared the approaching stripping disaster, a cell phone ringtone suddenly went off. Its melody loosened the tension between them.

Mikoto listened to it—it was different from her own ringtone.

"Kuroko…You still have all that useless stuff on your phone? Do you really need to have so many ringtones?"

"Heh-heh. And despite that, it's too small, too easy to lose, too hard to press the buttons, and too hard to see the screen." Shirai chuckled, exhausted, and took out her cell phone.

It, however, was vastly different from the general idea of what cell phones should be. It was cylindrical, like a tube of lipstick, one centimeter in diameter and five centimeters long. The actual part of it, clear and thin as a piece of paper, slid out from a slit on the side.

"That thing looks so futuristic, and yet it has no functionality at all," remarked Mikoto. "What a sham of a phone."

"Nobody asked you! I happen to like silly futuristic things. One day I want to ride a train that goes through a clear tube, too…Oh, excuse me for a moment, please."

Shirai turned her back to Mikoto. She looked at the screen, then put the actual phone part of it to her ear. It was a phone number in her contacts list. The numbers displayed on the screen belonged to an Academy City security group called Judgment, a police-like, anti-esper organization formed to solve problems in the city that Shirai belonged to.

"Yes, this is Shirai! I will have you know that I have finally gone shopping with Big Sister today and had just gotten to a good part. What could possibly be important enough to get in the way of that?"

"Wah…I'm relieved I was able to protect Miss Misaka's chastity."

The one on the phone was, of course, a colleague of hers from Judgment. The girl's voice was sweet like candy rolling around. Shirai considered immediately hanging up.

"Shirai, I ran into kind of a problem that a newcomer like me can't handle all alone. I'd like to get a veteran's opinion."

"You mean in terms of Level?"

"Uh-huh."

"Even though I am currently standing next to Big Sister and having the best time of my life?"

"Uh-huh. This really was an excellent coincidence in terms of timing. I'm surprised myself! Is this when I should laugh really loudly because I won? Wah-ha-ha-ha-ha!!"

Shirai slammed the cell phone microphone against a shop wall nearby.

"Ow?! M-my ears are ringing; the receiver's all weird..."

"If you make any more fun of me, I'll give you a nice present. How does nails on glass sound?"

"A-anyway, I'll be waiting at Branch 177. The situation is accelerating relatively quickly, so please come within thirty minutes."

Click. The girl hung up.

Kuroko Shirai sighed, putting back her cell phone. Regretfully, she turned back to Mikoto Misaka. "I do apologize for this, Big Sister. This is—Well, it is very difficult for me to say, but a rude idiot from Judgment has assigned me a job..."

"Don't worry about it. I'll see you off with my great big smile."

"...I could cry right now. I have no regrets. Please take care of yourself, Big Sister."

Shirai headed off for the bus terminal, her destination changed. She could use the last bus to cut down on time compared to walking through Academy City.

Then, suddenly, Mikoto said something. "Kuroko, I know you have to go do your job, but try your best to get back early tonight. The weather might go bad once night falls."

"Oh, I had not noticed. I forgot to check the weather report for today. Thank you very much. I will see you back at the dormitory, Big Sister."

Shirai gave a short bow, then turned around and headed for the bus terminal. She heard Mikoto's footsteps walking away, too, but those eventually faded.

Now worried about the look of the sky, she gazed upward. It didn't seem like it was going to rain, but—

Hm...?

She suddenly felt that something had been wrong with what Mikoto just said.

The weather might go bad once night falls.

At first, that might have sounded like an everyday thing to say. But among the three satellites Academy City had launched into space, one of them, the Tree Diagram, was supposed to be a perfect simulation machine. Weather forecasting was no exception. Her usage of the vague word *might* was not something you heard every day here.

That would mean Big Sister...

Bothered though she was by what Mikoto had said, she had her hands full dealing with the immediate problem. The last bus would depart in less than ten minutes. She adjusted her grip on her cheap bag and began an outright sprint toward her destination. Soon the little inconsistency had all but slipped her mind.

INTERLUDE ONE

Academy City's seventh school district.

In a corner of town in the same district as the Garden of Learning that lacked any of the school's brilliance, there was a student dormitory where a certain young man named Touma Kamijou lived.

It was a boys' dormitory, of course, but this one room was overlooked as an exception. There was a girl of fourteen or fifteen with long silver hair wearing a completely white habit rolling around on the floor. She was a freeloader.

The rolling Index was currently in complete control of the television.

The weather forecast was on. With a giant map of Japan in the background, a smiling lady in a suit was giving the clothes-drying index. They'd been doing the UV ray announcements until a few days ago. For the average high school student, Touma Kamijou, it had finally started to feel a little like the seasons were changing. (They were still in the midst of a heat wave lingering from summertime, though.)

"Touma, Touma! How do they know tomorrow's weather?" asked the sister without turning around. "All they have on the map are things that look like the rings in tree stumps."

Kamijou's exasperated voice came back from the one-room apartment's kitchen space. "Index, sit farther away from the television when you're watching it." He continued to drop the seasoned chicken meat into the oil. He was making fried chicken for dinner. "And those tree-ring things are called isobars. They can roughly figure out whether it'll be cloudy if they look at the atmospheric pressure on mountains and in valleys and stuff. Actually, sometimes clouds bump into mountains and make rain, so it's not all about the pressure."

"Huh. Wait, really? You can read calamities in geography...? Oh! I see! Academy City figured out how to do geomancy using artificial methods!!"

"You seem to be shaking all over in enjoyment, so I'll leave you alone. I'll talk to the cat instead. It's time for the deep-fried taste testing!"

Kamijou picked one of the freshly browned pieces out of the oil with tongs, set it on a small plate, and placed it on the floor. The calico, which had been curled up near Index, reacted immediately. Like an arrow springing from a bow, it shot over to the plate and started taking little bites, then rolling around as if to say, *Hot! It's hot but I'll still eat it! But it's hot!* and then coming back for more. He took out another plate and put some water on it. The cat must not have been wild before; someone had probably raised it. It wasn't even slightly cautious about hearing the sizzling sounds of something being fried nearby.

Index saw this and stood up vehemently from her spot in front of the television. "N-no fair. Whenever I snatch food like that, you get mad at me! You're giving Sphinx special treatment and it's not fair!"

"What? No, you eat literally *everything* whenever I take my eyes off you...Whoa, wait! That one's still not done! I only just seasoned the thing! Stop!!"

Skillfully using the metal tongs, Kamijou succeeded in a desperate defense of tonight's dinner, protecting it from the human vacuum cleaner coming at him at full force. In the meantime, a couple of the pieces started to burn. The hungry and angry nun Index clamped onto his head instead of the food.

Suddenly, she childishly cocked her head to the side. "Wait, Touma, sometimes the lady on the weather forecast says stuff that's not right. Is being a birdbrain her selling point?"

"I guess coming from *you*, she'd *have* to admit she was a birdbrain—*Ow*, hey!" he screamed in tandem with the chomping sound effect. "W-well, you know. Weather forecasts aren't perfect, even though they act like it. They used to be perfect, but it looks like their calculation equipment is broken."

"???"

Index seemed to have a mind full of questions, but Kamijou didn't go into the details.

The Tree Diagram.

The ultimate supercomputer. It could accurately predict the movement of every single particle of air on earth. It was one of the three satellites Academy City had launched into space—and it no longer existed in this world.

Kamijou glanced at the television.

The weather forecast, now without the perfect cogwheels behind it, ended, and the traffic report began with news of delays.

CHAPTER 2

Maidens in Opposition
Space_and_Point.

1

The school bus Kuroko Shirai got on was shared among all five schools in the Garden of Learning.

With the kind of finances the young ladies' schools possessed, they could have had separate buses, but they had put them together anyway. According to them, it was so that the students could experience a society that guaranteed the most safety possible.

Its size and gorgeous interior design had earned it the name of two-story parade bus. In fact, all the student seats were on the bottom, and the top floor was a big café lounge—that's how extravagant it was. Because of its size, it took the bigger roads and followed a course around the five student dormitories.

Kuroko Shirai didn't get off at the stop in front of Tokiwadai Middle School's dorm.

She alighted in front of a completely different dormitory, surrounded by girls from another school. She stretched her arms and sighed. Seriously, what about that bus was similar to "most societies" trying to *prevent* creating sheltered girls? Other types of buses—normal ones—stopped in front of Tokiwadai's dorm, too, and the difference between them was like night and day.

The time was half past seven in the evening.

During the summer, the sun would still be setting at this time, but now that it was mid-September, it was already dark out.

Shirai took her Judgment armband out of her bag and stuck it on her shoulder. Then she started in the opposite direction than all the girls around her. The flimsy bag felt more like baggage when she switched gears from "after school" to "on the job." Slowly and steadily, the number of combat-related items she kept in it was beginning to outnumber her school-related necessities.

Right next to the dormitory, she could see the building of another school.

Its totally normal, square, concrete walls marked it as completely different from those in the Garden of Learning. Shirai went in. She borrowed some little-used slippers from the staff entrance and headed into the hallway, lit here and there by lights. For a few moments, she plodded over the cold, hard linoleum and then found a door with a long-winded name on it: JUDGMENT OFFICER ACTIVITY BRANCH 177.

There was a glass plate next to the door. After it scanned her fingerprint, veins, and fingertips, the strict lock opened, and she threw open the door without knocking first. It made a loud *slam*.

The girl inside gave a sharp jolt. Her name was Kazari Uiharu. She was the same age as Shirai, but her short height and rounded shoulder lines made her look younger. It was rare to see a middle school student the summer sailor uniform *didn't* look right on, but Shirai felt that was the case here. Her hair was short and black, and she wore a decoration patterned with flowers like roses and hibiscus. From far away it would have looked like she had a colorful flower vase on her head.

Shirai, glancing at her fright, rudely stepped into Branch 177.

"What did you need? Judgment's a big organization, you know. Why did you have to call me for this?"

"Weeell, after thinking about it more, maybe it didn't absolutely *need* to be you, Shirai..."

"...You knew very well I was out shopping with Big Sister. If that's how you feel, then maybe you should change your attitude a little bit, hmm?"

"Hooraaaaay!"

"Not like that! Why are you waving your hands and acting so inspired?!"

Shirai teleported over to Uiharu in an instant and got the small girl's temples with her fists, then started twisting. She still had her bag on her arm, and its clasps bounced on Uiharu's ear.

They were both in their first year of middle school. They acted like one held a spot above the other, though, because of Tokiwa-dai's unique brand and the fact that Shirai was Level Four. Well, Shirai *had* rescued Uiharu, still not part of the organization, back on her first job as a member of Judgment, but Uiharu was the only one paying an undue amount of attention to that.

Branch 177 was a single room, situated in what was more like an office than a school. There were steel business desks in a row, like in city halls, and several computers.

Uiharu was facing one of those computers. She was sitting in an ergonomic chair that was soft and flabby like a Dali melting clock, whose rounded designs were scientifically proven to make it harder for the one sitting to grow tired. Shirai, giving her a noogie from behind, naturally looked up to the computer monitor.

It displayed what looked like a GPS map. There was a red X drawn on it—usually that meant something was going down. There were a few other points labeled on the map as well, and on another window she could see photographs and other data.

She would have to listen to Uiharu's explanation in order

to know what it meant—but she did have an impression just based on her broad glimpse of it all. "Oh, my. This isn't a school fight, is it?"

She wouldn't have been using GPS if it were a problem in a school setting. She would have brought a rough sketch of the school's floor plan.

Judgment was the collective disciplinary organization for schools; it generally existed to maintain peace and safety in school. There was a branch in each school in the city, and unlike police boxes, they didn't operate at all hours of the day. They'd be locked up as the last buses were leaving and emptied out—with today being an exception, apparently.

As long as they weren't in a state of emergency, Anti-Skill would be in charge of "extramural" peacekeeping activities. They couldn't leave dangerous streets or night patrols to students, after all—at least, that was the adults' point of view.

Shirai stopped grinding on the girl's temples and Uiharu's face relaxed a bit. "I contacted Anti-Skill like the manual says, but the situation is kind of odd. Anti-Skill seemed desperate for us to share our information with them right away, and I just thought you would be able to give better answers than I would, so...Oh, should I put on some tea or anything?"

"I'll pass, thank you. I would rather not pour tea into an empty stomach." Shirai considered tea to be something to enhance dishes and desserts, so she wasn't a big fan of anything that brought the tea itself into focus, like afternoon teatime.

Uiharu's face went blue with astonishment at her curt reply. She moaned, "But I've been spending so much time reading books on black tea to try and be more like a proper young lady! I even got kind of obscure spices like Japanese rose oil, too! And you evaded it with the kind of relaxed air proper young ladies have! But at school, we all yearn for black tea because it's an upper-class thing to do, right?!"

Tokiwadai Middle School and the young ladies who commuted there were the objects of adoration of every girl in Academy City. Most of them, however, didn't actually know anything about the lives of those who attended. Sometimes there would be girls who would be attracted by the prospect of going to a young ladies' school, then end up studying really weird stuff, like Uiharu here.

"Right. The only ones who get into it like that are people who just came into a lot of money. Anyway, what exactly seems to be the problem?"

"Well, I suppose I am still lower class—to me, that wouldn't matter because those people are still rich. Anyway, about the problem at hand, it's no big deal, really. It's like a robbery, or should I say a purse snatching. But ten people or so are attacking the victims. It's not what you could call efficient."

Mulling over that, Shirai put her flimsy bag on a nearby chair and focused on the monitor. It showed a map of District 7. The X was at the corner of a major road in front of a station. A few colored arrows were drawn from there toward nearby roads, indicating potential escape routes.

She looked at it dubiously. "That certainly doesn't seem like something we should have anything to do with."

"Well, this is where the problem starts. According to eyewitnesses, they stole a bag of carry-on luggage."

"Carry-on luggage???"

"Oh, you don't know, Shirai? It's a kind of bag—about as big as a suitcase, and it has wheels on the bottom," she explained briskly. "It always looks to me more like something a flight attendant might use rather than something one person would take on a trip. And the witnesses say the luggage had a tag on it."

"So basically, there was a tag on this travel bag? What's the problem with that?"

"Umm, well, look at this. Autonomous police robots caught it on camera, too, and I zoomed in and looked..." Uiharu hit a key and a new window opened. It showed numbers from the tag, its shipper, and its delivery address.

Shirai read the delivery address and frowned a bit. "Tokiwadai Middle School Calculation Support Facility...? I've never heard a name like that before."

"Oh, you haven't? It's hard to get in contact with the Garden of Learning, so it's hard to confirm one way or the other. I mean, even with the Daihasei Festival right around the corner, they're not opening it up to the public as part of the competitions, right?" asked Uiharu, sounding disappointed at that part in particular. "I checked the number on the tag, too, but it's weird. The number is registered, but it says its contents are a large cooling device made to prevent the overheating of a host computer that manages a grid of calculation devices. Something like that would never fit in carry-on luggage, right?"

"What...? Metal objects might be one thing, but I've never heard of anyone importing actual equipment into the Garden of Learning."

"I'm doing an analysis on the image of the tag itself; I don't have positive proof whether it's the real thing or not. It's probably a counterfeit tag someone copied and put on there for some reason."

"...Wait. All this talk of camera images and witnesses... Shouldn't you just be asking the person directly about what happened when their luggage was stolen? Wouldn't that be faster?"

"Said person isn't around." Shirai did a double take, surprised at Uiharu's quick response. She spoke again. "Apparently the victim is conducting his own pursuit, separate from us. See the image right before this? There were over ten robbers, and yet here, he's contacting someone and chasing on his own."

Uiharu typed something and brought up a new window in the mess of windows already on the screen. It was a vivid video recording. There was a rich-looking man wearing a suit at what seemed to be a road in front of a station. He looked around, then used a wireless radio instead of a cell phone and contacted someone.

"Right here," said Uiharu, suddenly pausing the video. "Do you notice anything strange?"

Shirai looked at the still image, but nothing particularly stood out to her. There was a slight blur on his face as she'd stopped the video right when the man in the suit with the wireless radio suddenly shook his head, so she couldn't make that out very well.

"Shirai, do you see how the victim's suit is turned up a little?"

"Huh. Well, now that you mention it." The ends of the man's suit were turned up slightly due to his movement. And near his side, she could see a blackish, suspender-like thing.

"You can make out the serial number if you enlarge it. L_Y010021. It's an official shoulder holster made by a big-name gun manufacturer. It's the kind for hiding a handgun inside your clothing. You know how on detective shows when the guy pulls a handgun out of his clothes? That's what it is," finished Uiharu, enlarging the holster's belt.

Shirai smiled a little. "It could just be an accessory."

"Yes. It may just be an accessory—and this could be, too." Uiharu did something. It zoomed in on the chest of the man in the suit, and hundreds of thin arrows appeared. It was detecting the subtle unevenness in the clothing. It looked like a magnet attracting iron filings. The innumerable arrows created the vague outline of a handgun. "That's all this image has to offer...It would have been nice to have some more pictures. What do you think, Shirai?"

Shirai thought. Was the man trying to avoid cameras? Or did he just happen to go out of sight as a result of chasing the fleeing robbers? "Good grief. I get the feeling this is going to be a huge pain, like always."

"Huh? Shirai, I didn't know you had farvision."

"Oh, be quiet. I can't say much for sure about the handgun with only this data, but the wireless radio—it looks like the professional kind I saw during Judgment training. Which means...I get it. It would appear these are some quite troubling circumstances. Even the fact that we didn't get a report is odd."

The victim was moving alone.

The carry-on luggage had something to do with Tokiwadai Middle School.

The things the man had on him seemed unnatural.

It was certainly different from your regular old incident. And if there really was a handgun involved, it would probably change what Anti-Skill would bring into it. At that point, Judgment would have no place in the incident (not every member of Judgment had reached Level Four power levels like Shirai had), so maybe having someone familiar with the Garden of Learning or Tokiwadai Middle School would help somewhat.

"So, Shirai...Between the culprits and the victim, which should we focus on getting information about?"

"I'd like to tell you to investigate both, but if I had to choose, it would be the ones who committed the robbery," she ordered, taking a step back. "If we recover the luggage, then the victim would eventually get to us without us having to chase him down. Do we know where the culprits fled? Well, I mean, it took me thirty minutes to get here, so I'm sure you don't know exactly where they are."

"That's not true," declared Uiharu simply. "After they stole the carry-on luggage, they apparently went into the underground mall on foot, without using a car or anything. I think it was probably to get somewhere out of satellite view."

"...? To escape our sight? It isn't like the underground is completely devoid of cameras. They're set up all over, and there're autonomous robots patrolling the place, too."

"Yes, but it is still easier to flee there than above ground. Without the bird's-eye view from the satellite, he could blend in with

the other people there and fool the cameras. And sometimes it's faster to run through the underground, too. There's currently congestion on the main lines in the area—#3, #48, #131—due to an electricity mishap to the traffic signals or something. And using a car would be particularly hopeless. Running in the underground would give both speed and stealth."

"Is that right?" Shirai nodded.

Anti-Skill, having received word from Shirai, was probably moving now as well. Any wheeled vehicles would find themselves stuck in the traffic, though. Considering they didn't know how much importance to assign to this incident, it would take too long to go through paperwork to get a helicopter or the like. The many processes were to prevent individual troops from requisitioning equipment for personal use, but of course, organizations always came with the side effect of being inflexible.

"Jeez. I suppose it would be best to go there posthaste."

"Ehh?! If you're not here, Shirai, then I'll have to give Anti-Skill an answer on my own!" complained Uiharu, truly against the idea. "That will be such a pain!"

Shirai gave her a dull stare. "You needn't worry about a thing. I'll go clean up the *pain* right now." She took her flimsy bag from the chair it was on and headed for the entrance. Without turning around, she said, "Just who do you think I am? Above ground, underground—it doesn't matter to me."

2

Kuroko Shirai possessed an ability called teleportation.

It wasn't an all-powerful skill, though. The weight limit of what she could teleport was 130.7 kilograms, and its max range—regardless of the weight of the object—was 81.5 meters. Plus, she could only use the power on things she touched. She couldn't bring something far away to her.

On the other hand, though, that meant she had no trouble moving the constant reference point of the ability: herself.

Shoom, shoom, came the sounds splitting the air, over and over again.

Every time she warped eighty meters, she'd designate her next destination eighty more meters away and jump again. Others would have been seeing her at a place, then not seeing her, then seeing her again somewhere else. Of course, it was far faster than traveling by foot. Translating it into velocity would mean she was reaching 288 kilometers a second.

I'm not moving in a straight line; I'm moving from point to point, she said to herself, crossing space again. *Luckily that means inertia has nothing to do with it. It would be no joke if I were to be affected by air resistance while wearing this skirt.*

She changed her foothold every jump, leaping from roads to railings to the tops of vending machines. There were voices of surprise around her, but they were espers all the same. It didn't evolve into an especially big ruckus, probably because not only did she wear a Tokiwadai uniform but also a Judgment armband.

In contrast to the robbers running underground, Shirai was flying around above ground. But the underground mall had a limited number of entrances, so as long as she accurately held them, they wouldn't get by her. In fact, if she were to carelessly pursue them underground and drive them down mentally, they could end up inciting violence among the civilians down there. (It was still unknown as to whether they possessed weapons, but even barehanded, ten people were a pretty big threat to civilians.) Thinking sensibly, there were only so many entrances to the underground mall, so if chaos broke out, it would be harder to evacuate the civilians. She needed to approach this delicately and from above ground.

If she was going to arrest them, it would have to be somewhere with not a lot of people *and* above ground. On top of that, it would be best if she could control the situation so she could finish it swiftly and surgically.

Then her cell phone rang.

Shirai took it in her hand, not breaking her teleportation chain. A buzzing, staticky sound came out. She was instantly crossing space, so with the radio-wave receiver constantly changing places, things went wrong.

"Shira—i, the culprits—moving…They came out—from the entran—A03 of—Area Sale mall—They seem to be going—from the end of the underground mall to the next one…"

She gave a single phrase in response. "I already see them." She hung up and returned the phone to her pocket.

Near a building that looked like a subway entrance, she spotted people weaving through a mob of cars laid out like bricks. The cars' horns were blaring, but all the suit-wearing men kept on going. She saw one of them pulling a wheeled white carry-on luggage behind him. They had evidently been *trying* to keep things covert, and now they seemed somehow ashamed as they crossed the large roadway and entered a narrow alley.

Shirai made sure she had a good grip on her bag, and *bam!* She took off, noticeably more powerfully this time.

The next moment, she was already in the alley. Right in the middle of the ten or so men. She exchanged glances with the man with the carry-on luggage and gave him a smile. Before he could be surprised at all, she was running a finger along the surface of the luggage.

Teleport.

She disappeared again, then reappeared at the end of the alley to prevent their exit. Beside her was the white luggage, which she'd taken with her when she crossed through space.

She put one hand on her hip and touched the other to the luggage. "Excuse me, I am with Judgment. I expect I do not have to explain why I came here?"

Her voice was condescending, depending on how one listened to it.

And so the men reacted swiftly. Each one reached into his suit's breast pocket and brought out a black handgun, each with the same design. Just looking at them struck her with a hefty weight.

Crap, so they weren't just some regular old purse-snatchers! When did this turn into a spy movie?!

Shirai crouched down behind the carry-on luggage to use it as a shield, but they seemed confident. Their index fingers didn't hesitate on the triggers—they would aim precisely for the parts of her sticking just a little bit out from her "shield." Her throat made a very slight and unnatural sound. Her teleportation wasn't responsive or precise enough to send away every single bullet.

Fire flared from the ten muzzles.

But Shirai was crossing through space just one step faster. She was aiming to get behind the man in the back.

Kuroko Shirai and the carry-on luggage disappeared. She left only her flimsy bag behind in midair; after a moment it plopped straight to the ground.

The men seemed bewildered, their target suddenly having vanished. Meanwhile, Shirai took the giant carry-on luggage with both hands and gave a really hard wallop to the guy all the way in the back.

"Gah…!" he groaned. The other thieves all started to turn around at once. Shirai touched one of them and teleported. The man immediately changed places—but only by a few centimeters, and with his body turned all the way around.

What ended up happening was that eight men spun to look behind them, and one of them instead turned to glare at *them*.

The thieves were now all pointing their guns at one another like a Mexican standoff.

"Uh." The man who had gotten turned around hurriedly pointed his away, and that was when Shirai delivered a massive kick to his back. The robbers all fell to the ground like dominoes. She swung the carry-on luggage up with all her might, then brought it down on each of the gun-wielding men's wrists in turn. There was a series of short shrieks. They couldn't run—they couldn't move. It was like they were wrapped in spider thread. If they tried to use their guns, they'd probably have to go through their own piled-up allies. As a result, despite all their murderous weapons, each one only waited helplessly to be knocked out and lose consciousness.

"Well, that was nothing to write home about. In fact, it was a little *too* easy for my tastes," she said derisively, though to no response.

She poked the men with her toes to make sure they were all unconscious, then bound them all in Judgment's nonmetal handcuffs. She ran out after the first four, so she made use of a loose cable lying on the ground. Despite the pressure on their wrists, none of them woke up.

After giving Anti-Skill a quick call, Shirai glanced at their equipment.

She looked at the name and model number of their guns, but she didn't understand them. She knew they were completely different from the ones they'd held during Judgment training, though. The main pieces of handguns developed by Academy City weren't made with metal and were thus extremely light. These men's guns, though, were hunks of steel. There were numbers and English letters engraved on their sides. She briefly wondered if they were their official model numbers, but that was all. She didn't have much technical knowledge regarding the armaments—Anti-Skill, which fought mainly with firearms, was one thing, but she used her ability for combat.

Aside from that, she couldn't find any identification on the suit-wearing men. It looked like they might have purposely erased them. She looked at the face of one of the fallen men and clicked her tongue in annoyance. "...Gold teeth?" she muttered dubiously at the wide-open mouth of the unconscious man. There were a number of better materials for that job in Academy City. Nobody used gold teeth in this city these days.

She found cell phones with no registered numbers in the pockets of their slacks, but they were old as well. Academy City didn't sell any of this stuff.

It was said that Academy City's internal technology level was twenty or thirty years removed from the outside world. Electronics went without saying, but even smaller articles that wouldn't appear to have anything to do with "technology" sometimes looked different here.

They were trained to a certain extent, given the way they held their guns, but they were completely led on by my ability, so it must have been the first time for them...Perhaps they do not have any ties to espers at all and are professionals from the outside.

"..."

And now for the carry-on luggage. Those outsiders had sneaked all the way into Academy City to get their hands on it. She looked down at it once again.

It was large. Like other travel luggage, it was rectangular in shape. If she curled up, she could probably fit inside the thing. It was white, and its surface was made from a special material with a glossy finish, like it had been waxed or something.

She put a hand to the latches keeping it closed—to no avail. "Locked...I suppose I should have expected that."

But upon surveying it again, she realized the lock was extremely elaborate. There were two physical locks, one electronic one, and even a magnetic lock, which was said to have a practically infinite number of patterns.

"Well, none of that matters to my ability."

Her ability was teleportation. She couldn't move something unless she touched it, so she couldn't take an object out of a box.

However, if she moved only the box itself, she could get the contents that way.

She couldn't move really heavy "boxes" like the ones in bank vaults, but a piece of luggage wouldn't be that difficult. She casually held her right hand out to the luggage, then placed her fingers on its surface.

Huh?

Then she noticed it.

This case had essentially no gaps in the outside. Something like rubber packing was stuffed into various places, as if to make it waterproof. All of the gaps in it were shielded.

Wait…Is whatever is inside sensitive to light? Like photography film?…It must be something delicate. Oh, and there I went, slapping those men silly with it. She thought for a moment, then came to a quick conclusion. *I suppose putting off opening it would be for the best. I will have a clairvoyant or mind-reading colleague check it first,* she decided as she scrutinized it, put off by its excessive shielding.

Suddenly, though, she spotted some kind of tape stuck to its side, as though it were keeping its cover on. It was the tag from before. It was printed elaborately and reminded her of paper money. There was probably an IC chip embedded in it somewhere, too.

The things written on it were the same as what Uiharu had shown her earlier. They wouldn't be able to distinguish it without putting it through a machine, but at the very least, none of it seemed strange to her eyes.

What's this marking…? Shirai looked down the side of the luggage again. There was a marking engraved directly into the case, separate from the tag. It was a simple mark, with a few rectangular shapes overlapping inside a circle. She felt like she'd seen it somewhere before, but she couldn't remember exactly where.

She decided to stop thinking about it. "Best to ask others what

I don't understand, I suppose." She took her cell phone out of her skirt pocket, then removed the super-thin scroll-looking part out of the small tube. She then used its camera to snap a picture of the entire carry-on luggage, the tag, and the marking, sending it all in a message to Uiharu with only the words *look at please.*

Sure enough, one hundred twenty seconds later, she got a response. Shirai hit the talk button before the second note in her ringtone could play.

"Shiraaai, it's Uiharu. You finished your job, so I have a report for you and a demand for a prize."

"I'll accept the report but not your demand," she answered smoothly, though inside she was astonished at Uiharu's investigative prowess—she didn't let it into her voice, though. She might have had access privileges to the city's data banks, but her response time was insane.

"Demands are demands because you have to demand them! Well, anyway, I'll give you my report first. That carry-on luggage is special, basically. It's really airtight and blocks all kinds of cosmic rays. See how the surface is gleaming like that?"

Now that she mentions it, thought Shirai, looking at the luggage's surface. It was like it was waxed. It reflected light, showing Shirai's own face.

"It looks like the really good stuff they use in astronaut suits and the outside of space shuttles. And obviously, given the technology used to make it, it was created in Academy City."

"Wait, cosmic rays…What for?"

"Just how it sounds. You don't need much in the way of protection from cosmic rays when you're on Earth. Though I can't say for sure, since the ozone layer has been doing badly lately."

Which means…Outer space, so…Were they going to use this in some kind of EV work in space?

The unexpected development gave her alarm.

"Next is the tag. Oh, but before that…Shirai, I have a request.

Can you change your phone to RWS mode and take another picture of the tag? There's a red square on the right side of it. Focus on that."

"What? RWS mode?"

"It's the mode you put it in to read electronic data from IC chips and stuff! It's standard issue on all Judgment cell phones. I put that expansion chip in your cell phone for you, remember?! You haven't even read the manual, have you?!"

"I know basically how to use a cell phone, so I never felt like going through the minor things in the manual…"

"Ahh, jeez! Anyway, first, open the main menu…"

Shirai followed Uiharu's directions and came to a screen she'd never seen before on her cell phone. Then she took a picture of the tag again. She attached it to a message and sent it to Uiharu.

"Oh, there we go! Got it! Umm, let's see what the scan says… Yep, it found something." Uiharu's tone changed to one of seriousness. "The tag itself is the real thing, and it was definitely issued by Academy City."

"The real thing…Then it was going to the Garden of Learning like we thought?"

"Yes."

Shirai began to think. There was no building at Tokiwadai Middle School called the "Calculation Support Facility." By nature, if a nonexistent delivery address was written on a package's tag, there wouldn't be any point in delivering it. That meant this sort of message might actually have been some sort of code that would mean something to somebody else.

"The analysis on the IC chip info finished, too. It supplements the simple type of code printed on the tag. It has the frame number of a space shuttle and an outer space work schedule number. Both belong to Academy City. They match the records of District 23. This is smelling more and more like danger!"

"District 23…The whole thing is covered in airfields and launch sites for aviation and space research and development; nowhere else in the city has facilities like that. Students aren't allowed in there."

"Yes. And that mark on the luggage? The one with the squares inside the circle. That's District 23's emblem. It's kind of like a school insignia."

Shirai groaned. Part of her wondered why she didn't realize that earlier, but she wouldn't generally have remembered the emblem for a facility with no connection to students. She'd probably glanced at it before on the news during space shuttle launches or something.

"The sender on the tag is also District 23," continued Uiharu. "Everything there is highly classified, so there's no sensitive details written on it, of course."

Shirai looked at the bag again. The date matched the date Academy City's shuttle returned to Earth. And the shipper was District 23—an airfield-slash-launch-site monopolizing an entire school district for aviation and space research.

Who in the world did District 23 plan on delivering the luggage to…? she wondered. *And who could those guys who stole it out from under them have been…?* For now, she decided to just thank Uiharu. "Thank you. I will give it some thought while I deal with the luggage and these men."

"Ahh! Like I said before, I expect a reward! Like a proper young ladies' teatime with a real lady like you! Actually, not just tea! It has to have the atmosphere that only proper ladies craft!!"

She sounded quite flustered. Shirai hung up anyway.

Like a scroll being rolled up, she watched as the super-thin phone was wound back up into the cylinder holding it. Then she returned it to her pocket and started giving some more thought to this.

Unfortunately, Shirai didn't have much knowledge of space-related technology or events.

Even when she thought it over, the only space-related happening she could think of happening recently was the continuous schedule of rocket and shuttle launches by organizations all over the world, beginning with Academy City.

"It might be...a bit of a stretch to connect this to that. Still... Sheesh. After all that, I still don't even know whether I should look inside this thing or not." She sighed and sat down on the luggage. The men in the suits were a mystery, but then so was the one who had been carrying this in the first place. "Either way, it is not my job to think about it any more than this."

Having come to a noncommittal conclusion, she waited there for Anti-Skill to arrive. They were taking a while, though the road conditions were not very good. Shirai wouldn't complain, though—they didn't have any abilities, so they couldn't help it.

Then, her cell phone suddenly rang.

She looked at the tiny screen and saw the words *Mikoto Misaka* written on it. She quickly turned back toward the men. They were still out cold, but she wanted to avoid carelessly letting them overhear her conversation and trying to start trouble. Leaving the scene for a personal matter would be an issue, though. Though feeling a slight resistance to doing so, she brought her hand to her mouth as if telling someone a secret and pushed the talk button on her cell phone.

"Hey, Kuroko?...I'm not getting very good reception. Where are you, anyway?"

"Um, err, well...I sort of can't say where I am."

"Huh? Oh, okay, I got it. Still on the job...Sorry for bothering you!"

"No, not at all. What did you need?"

"No, if you're working, then don't worry about it. The underclassmen are saying we should definitely be on the lookout for a surprise R.A. inspection, so I wanted you to hide your things if you could."

"??? Big Sister, are you not currently at the dormitory?"

"Um. Well, no. I can ask someone else. Do you mind them cleaning up your things?"

"Wha, what? What did you say...?! B-Big Sister, are you asking some other girl for a favor...? Please, wait, Big Sister! I will come back to the dorm as soon as possible, therefore, please, give to me the privilege of you saying what a good girl I am and giving me a hug!!"

"...Why would I hug you for something like this? Besides, you're working, aren't you? They're saying the rain should start around midnight, so if you don't want that, then hurry up and get your assignment done so you can go home. Bye!"

She hung up on her.

Shirai stared at the cell phone for a few moments as though she'd been left behind. A low ring of disappointment sounded in her mind—

Ka-thunk.

She heard soft footsteps.

Whoops. I was so absorbed in fighting that I never put up any off-limits tape, she thought vaguely, still sitting on the luggage.

Then, a moment later.

The sensation of her weight being supported by it disappeared. It just slipped away. She stuck out her hand, but it wasn't there. The luggage she had just been sitting on was no longer even within arm's reach.

It was like it had suddenly disappeared.

Almost like it had been teleported.

Tele...portation...

Shirai's mind was still somewhat blank after the unexpected event. She knew something was happening around her right now, but her thoughts couldn't catch up to it. Just when she managed to grasp that she was in danger...

Thud!

Something cut into her right shoulder as she lay there on the ground faceup.

"Gah…!"

There was a searing pain. She felt something inside her tearing apart. Not with her ears—the sharp noise was coming directly through her body.

She glanced and saw a pointed piece of metal stuck through the fabric of her short-sleeve blouse and into her skin. Its tip was like a thick wire and was twisted like a spring, and the handle was made of a white material that resembled porcelain.

A wine corkscrew?!

Kuroko Shirai forced her mind to be calm—the pain had almost taken over—and teleported. She only shifted a few centimeters, turning her fallen body up ninety degrees. As a result, she stood up instantly.

Drip, drop. The heavy sound of liquid splashing on the ground.

A pair of eyes watched in amusement.

Kuroko Shirai looked at the entrance to the alley again.

There was a girl there.

She was a little taller than her, and her hair was tied up into two long strands in the back. She was wearing a school uniform, but it was a winter one. She didn't have her arms through the sleeves of her long-sleeve blue blazer, instead wearing it over her shoulders, none of its buttons done. She wasn't wearing a blouse underneath it. Her torso was naked, with only some sort of light pink–colored bandage-like innerwear wrapped around her chest. She wore a belt at her waist, too. It wasn't there to hold up her skirt; it was just for decoration. It was made of metal plates linked together rather than leather. On it was a key ring that had a black, metal cylinder hanging from it, about forty centimeters long and three in diameter. It looked like a military-grade flashlight you might see on police officers.

Shirai somehow expected her to be in high school. She couldn't rely on her outward appearance to tell her age, but high school kids just looked older to middle school students. Something about her didn't give Shirai the impression that they were alike.

The girl had the white luggage next to her.

The one that Shirai had just been sitting on a moment ago.

"So it *was* teleportation?! But..." She hadn't touched the luggage. Or maybe she'd immediately teleported behind her and then went back with it. Even then...

If this is just teleportation, then something's wrong, she thought, alarmed.

Shirai, buried in thought, snapped out of it when she heard the girl laugh. "Oh, you figured it out already? I should have known an esper with a similar ability would be quick on the uptake. I'm a little different from your type, though."

Shirai frowned. A similar ability. A little different.

"My power—it's called Move Point. Unlike your shabby ability, my movement doesn't need me to touch the object. Amazing, ain't it?" That dispassionate voice...The girl looked down at the suit-wearing men on the ground behind Shirai. "These people were useless. That's why I assigned them this random job to grab the luggage. I didn't expect them to be so useless they couldn't even do *that*, though."

Useless. People. Grab. Random job. Assigned. Those words all clued Shirai in to the fact that she was somehow related to these men. She raised her voice and cautioned her. "You would commit violence against me despite knowing who I am?" The armband displaying her position was already bloodstained from the wound in her shoulder and turning black.

"Yes. That is exactly why I could be so calm with this, Miss Kuroko Shirai of Judgment. If I hadn't, I wouldn't have revealed my hand so easily."

Shirai didn't know what was in the luggage. And she didn't

know what this person was after, either. But she still understood; this girl, looking at her wounded state and laughing, wasn't about to let her go home quietly.

An enemy.

Yes, this was not a girl standing before her, but an enemy.

"Gah!!"

Shirai spread her feet wide. The recoil caused her short skirt to flutter. Her exposed thighs revealed leather belts around them, with dozens of metal darts inserted in each one—just like bullets in a gunman's belt in a western film. They were her trump card. Deadly darts that she could instantly warp to a target with teleportation and send into an enemy.

But the girl moved before Shirai was able to.

Her slender hand inside the blazer hanging from her shoulders went to the military-grade flashlight packed on her metallic belt and pulled it out in one breath. She spun it around in her hand like a baton, then waggled it just a tiny bit above Shirai, as though beckoning.

A change occurred.

The men Shirai had brought down and arrested vanished and warped in front of the girl. She held the ten unconscious people out in the air as a shield.

However…

"That won't help!!"

Shirai fired the metal darts at her thighs anyway. The numerous darts crossed space soundlessly, ignoring the linear distance in between them and the target—in other words, passing right through the men—and reappeared directly where the girl was standing. She was aiming for her shoulders and legs, firing carefully so she wouldn't hit her joints.

Her teleportation ability didn't move things in a straight line but rather from one position to another. There could be as many hostages in between them as she wanted; it didn't pose a problem.

And when the darts all appeared out of nowhere inside the girl's body, they would tear through her tender flesh from the inside out. The attack didn't depend on the type of object. For teleportation, the object being moved would appear overlapping the object she sent it to.

So it would have been odd if her attack didn't pierce the girl's body.

And yet…

"Uh," she grunted without meaning to.

After the men in the air succumbed to gravity and crumpled all over the place…

The girl wasn't there, where she'd expected.

She had taken a few steps back and was now sitting on the luggage, legs crossed elegantly. She had kicked it backward while sitting down so it skidded across the ground like a wheel.

All the darts Shirai fired hung in empty space for a moment, then they all clattered to the ground—just like the unconscious men had.

Teleportation was movement between points. If she designated the coordinates a little bit wrong, her attack wouldn't hit. The men hadn't been used as armor to block it but as a screen to throw off Shirai's perception.

The girl, legs still crossed, moved the flashlight in her hand. She pointed to one of the fallen darts with it, then flung it upward like a fishing rod.

One of the darts then vanished—and reappeared in the girl's empty hand.

Here it co—!!

The girl sidearmed the metal dart toward Shirai, busy preparing herself. She hadn't used teleportation (or Move Point, like she said). It was traversing a linear, three-dimensional route. It was, however, aimed precisely at the middle of Shirai's body.

She couldn't dodge it to the side given the width of the alley.

There was always the option of teleporting across a wall and into a building to flee, but she couldn't use it carelessly—she didn't know what the inside looked like. If she accidentally sent herself into coordinates overlapping with another person, it would be a terrible tragedy.

But there was no point in retreating backward. The dart was heading straight for her.

Therefore, she chose to teleport forward. She warped right in front of the girl, ending up on the other side of the dart. She balled a hand into a fist. It would be a counterattack—delivered right after evading an incoming attack, it would send her enemy flying. But before she could...

Smack.

A metal dart struck her in the flank from behind.

"...Ah...?!"

Shirai felt something like a tremble bubbling up from the core of her body. Quickly losing the ability to endure it, she felt all of her strength drain from her. Her legs buckled and she fell to the ground.

And oddly enough, it now looked like she was groveling at the girl's feet as she sat on the luggage.

"I already told you," she said with a smile, re-crossing her legs. "My Move Point doesn't need me to touch the object like yours does."

Kuroko Shirai heard her scornful tones—but couldn't get herself to lift her head up.

It was simple logic.

First, the girl had thrown a metal dart with her hand. Then, at the same time Shirai dodged it, she used Move Point on the flying arrow. To make it appear inside Shirai's back.

The metal dart had been skillfully flipped one-eighty degrees without it losing its momentum and had stuck farther into Shirai, toward her stomach, then finally stopped. A terrible scraping resounded from deep within her.

Shoom, shoom! The sound of air parting occurred in succession.

The next thing she knew, the girl's empty hand now held every single one of the metal darts Shirai dropped.

"How unfortunate for you. You're from Tokiwadai Middle School, yeah? Mikoto Misaka might be at her wits' end right now, but I didn't peg her as the type to get her subordinates and juniors wrapped up in her personal affairs. Well, I guess she didn't stop that experiment by herself, either, so maybe she doesn't care anymore."

Those words sent a jolt through Kuroko Shirai's body.

It wasn't a shudder of pain that went through her near-senseless body but a different kind of tremor. "What...was that?" She strained her neck. She lifted her head up. She gritted her teeth, rallied all her strength, and looked up as if beseeching the heavens from the ground below. "Why...would you mention...Big Sister's name?"

The girl decided to humor her and answer—as though to scorn her as no longer requiring caution, as her wounded state presented no threat. She seemed to enjoy watching how frustrated Shirai was, seeking pointless amusement at the expense of discarding the most logical course of action. "Oh?" Still cross-legged, the girl put a hand to her mouth as though this were a joke. "You didn't know? Well, it doesn't *seem* like you're being used without knowing it...Tokiwadai's Railgun doesn't have that kind of character."

She hadn't answered her.

Shirai had asked that question with the last of her strength, and all she got was a self-satisfied soliloquy.

"Didn't you think things were a little *too* convenient? Like how the useless person who stole this practically aimed to get wrapped up in a traffic jam? You couldn't guess the reason behind the electricity failure on the traffic lights? There's no possible way you wouldn't know what kind of powers Tokiwadai's ace has."

Kuroko Shirai glared, though she couldn't look above her.

She glared at the unidentified piece of luggage and the enemy reigning supreme atop it.

"What...have you..." Her dry lips clung together; she moved them anyway, coughing the words out as though blood would come out with them. The lip balm she'd borrowed from Mikoto sent a strangely sticky feeling back to her. "...been talking... about...?"

"The remnant—well, you wouldn't know just from my saying that. And 'silicon-corundum' would be difficult, too, I suppose," answered the girl, pleased, clanking the metal darts in her hand together. "Let's see. Perhaps if I mentioned the remnant of the Tree Diagram, you'd understand. It was broken, it was forgotten—and yet enormous possibility still remained within the super-computer's silicon-corundum central calculation unit."

Kuroko Shirai was shocked. "That's...impossible. Isn't it...up in satellite orbit...as we speak...?"

It was so absurd she didn't have a sense if it was real. The Tree Diagram, the world's finest simulation machine and the pride of Academy City, was being kept safely in space on board a satellite. Even if you wanted to do something to it, you would never be able to touch it so long as you were connected to the ground. Besides, if there had been an accident (or it had been destroyed), it would have had a pretty extensive round on the news.

However.

The luggage the girl sat on was made to be used in extra-vehicular work in space.

And its tag had the day Academy City's shuttle returned on it.

Agencies all over the world were currently competing for space advancement.

Shirai's thoughts wavered. The girl took a photograph out of her skirt pocket and flicked it toward her, spinning like a Frisbee. It fell in front of her. "An appendix to Academy City's report on its destruction. Rare, huh?"

The photograph showed the giant Earth against the deep-black background of space. In the foreground of the blue planet's gentle curves floated the scattered wreckage of a satellite. A satellite whose silhouette she had seen before on the news and in pamphlets.

"That...that's..."

As she stared in mute amazement, the photograph vanished, warping to between the girl's index and middle fingers. She'd used Move Point or whatever it was to get it. "The Tree Diagram was destroyed quite a while back. That's why everyone wants to get their hands on the remnants of the broken satellite floating around up there." She seemed to see something in Shirai's expression. "Mikoto Misaka sure has it rough. Someone blew up the Tree Diagram for her, so her nightmare ended—but now they're saying they're going to repair it. If that happens, they'll redo the experiment. So, well, I suppose I can sort of relate to her feeling she needs to struggle desperately against that."

At the mention of that one name from the girl's mouth, Shirai's abdominal muscles clenched.

Mikoto Misaka.

Why does she keep bringing her up? she thought. She had no way of knowing. She couldn't digest even a small piece of this situation. The girl turned a much stronger glare on her then. It was enough of an issue that such a dangerous person had so much as mentioned her anyway.

"Heh-heh. My, my! Seems you've been left out of the loop. By the looks of it, you don't even know anything about the experiment. But you've caught a glimpse of fragments of it. For example...yes, do you remember a couple weeks ago when there was that terrible explosion at the train switchyard? It held up every train in the city for a while. Huge mess. I recall being quite impressed by the skill with which you all got the train schedules back to normal in under a *week*."

The girl spoke pleasantly; Shirai couldn't answer. There was a sizzling impatience in her head, but she still didn't understand what this girl was saying.

"Still don't get it? I've said so much already. August twenty-first. Anything particularly odd happen around you that day?"

The girl could ask, but it was just a vague date. Shirai couldn't clearly picture it. Besides, the 21st of last month hadn't been a special day or anything. *What has she been saying...? Was I foolish to think I could even have a conversation with her?* Dubious though she was, the girl's words did seem to have some kind of regularity to them.

"I see. You made it so far that I would have gladly been your friend, you know," she said.

Shirai didn't have the strength to answer. Her lips were dry and slightly torn, the taste of blood dripping into her mouth.

She did understand two things, though.

First, that she needed to stop this girl right here and right now.

Second, that she couldn't allow the contents of the luggage to be given to anyone.

With one hand, she removed the scant few darts she had left on the belt on her thigh up her skirt. There were only two. She grasped them so tightly she almost crushed them, and then, as if to inspire herself, looked up to the sky and uttered a meaningless cry.

The girl never got up from her luggage. Legs still elegantly folded in front of her, toying with all the clinking darts in her hand, she flipped the switch on her military-grade flashlight—which could have also been used like a police baton—and spun it around, tracing a ring of light in the air. Then she looked down at the weakling groveling and struggling and writhing at her feet with tender-hearted ridicule.

There was a moment of silence.

The sound of a car engine ran by from outside the alley's exit, on the main road.

Both girls took that as their cue to act.

Not even a second was needed to decide the outcome.

Tons of metal needles flew through the air, scattering clear, fresh maiden blood. There was a scream.

With a wet *thump* of filthy clothes falling, Kuroko Shirai dropped to the ground.

The wind blew. There was no follow-up attack. The other girl left the alley, leaving the Judgment officer there.

She trotted along with light steps as though pleased, not bothering to use Move Point.

With the luggage.

B-Big...Sister...

In her frustration, she gritted her teeth and apologized in her mind. She couldn't possibly muster the strength to say it out loud.

She'd known what she had to do—her goals.

And yet the inexperienced Kuroko Shirai couldn't accomplish a single one.

INTERLUDE TWO

In the hospital, there was a bathroom with a bath in it used for in-patients.

In her green jersey, the gym teacher Aiho Yomikawa rested her back against the door to the bathroom. She was stylish and pretty enough that wearing a jersey seemed almost sacrilegious. Her breasts jutting out of the front even surrounded the simple jersey with a tremendous appeal. The fact that she didn't realize its worth at all portrayed her as even more dangerously unprotected.

Stupid Kikyou, giving me more weird problems to deal with! She sighed, reminded again of the face of her old friend, a female researcher currently in the hospital. During the one instance Yomikawa had been allowed to see her, all the researcher told her was to look after a certain pair of children. The requester fell unconscious right after making her request, leaving Yomikawa with no details and no way to refuse.

Apparently she'd been entrusted with a unique duo of espers.

She could hear the children's voices from the other side of the door—from in the bathtub.

"Splish-splash-splish-splash-splish-splash goes Misaka goes Misaka, doing a flutter kick in the narrow bathtub. Maybe this is indoor leisure particularly made for tiny bodies, suggests Misaka suggests Misaka, exploring new possibilities."

"Shit, you're getting water in my face! You're not supposed to swim around the freakin' bathtub!!"

"If only you could use your reflection, says Misaka says Misaka, giving you a pitiful look. Still, the strongest esper starts crying when he gets shampoo in his eyes, huh, says Misaka says Misaka, astonished."

"I haven't completely lost my reflection. I can't get all bossy with it, since I'm using your network to do the calculations, though. But if I used it here, all the water would bounce off my skin and I might as well have not come here in the first place…Also, I'm not crying, the shampoo in my eyes doesn't hurt a bit! It might be the first time I ever got the damn thing in my eyes but it doesn't matter!"

"Splish-splash-splish-splash-splish-splash!"

"Yomikaaaaaawaaaaaaaaaa!! Why?! Why do I need to suffer through this brat's fucking thrashing in here?!"

Oh, they're talking to me now. Yomikawa raised her eyebrows. "It's fiiine! It's dangerous for little kids to go unsupervised in the bathtub. They could drown, 'kay?"

"Then why don't you supervise her?!"

"It's fiiine! If I had to play with such a rambunctious kid, I'd get all soaked and see-through, y'know? Besides, you need to wash yourself properly now that you can finally take a bath again, 'kay?"

"This is bullshit…!! Why am I constantly surrounded by people who lack the mental faculties to listen to what I'm saying, damn it?!"

"There, there, there, comforts Misaka comforts Misaka. I understand this is embarrassing for you, but as you can see, Misaka is Misaka is properly equipped with a bath towel. Paying too much attention to it will make things harder for you, says Misaka says Misaka, offering some life advice."

"Yeah, right. Here, I'll give you a shower to the face as thanks."

"Bfpppft?! says Misaka says Misaka, toppling over at the sudden attack! That was rude—you risked your life to stand up for me at the end of summer, says Misaka says Misaka, her face going white!"

"Hah?…Wait a second!"

"You were so kind to me when the virus was destroying me, so why are you acting like this to me now—could you be bored of Misaka already?! asks Misaka asks Misaka, trembling and shivering at the possibility!"

"…Uh? What did you just say?…The virus?"

"Oh no, says Misaka says Misaka, clamping a hand over her mouth."

"Don't *oh no* me, you brat! How do you remember what happened that day?!"

"Umm, says Misaka says Misaka, poking her cheek with her index finger and stuff."

"You were supposed to lose all your memories when I fixed the fucking virus in your brain!"

"Misaka shares her memories with all the Misakas in the network, from #10032 to #20000, admits Misaka admits Misaka."

"…I see."

"Basically, I guess if one Misaka loses her memories, it's okay, since she has a backup, says Misaka says Misaka, sticking out her tongue cutely. They're not Misaka's memories, but I can get them back by absorbing memories from other Misakas again, says Misaka says Misaka, making all sorts of gestures in a frantic, solitary battle to quell your rage and stuff."

"Okay…so what? Do you know what I shouted on that day—?"

" 'Yeah, I killed ten thousand of those Sisters. But that's not reason to let the other ten thousand die. Ah, jeez, I know that sounds whitewashed. I know the words coming out of my mouth right now! But you're wrong! We may be the epitome of human trash, but no matter what your reason is, there's no fucking way it's okay to kill that kid!'…says Misaka says Misaka, the memory bringing a tear to her eye."

"You…you fucking brat…I'm gonna kill you…!!"

"It's fiiine! Besides, a friend of mine left her to me, so don't give me any more work to do, okay?" said Yomikawa vaguely, listening to the two of them splashing water at each other in negotiation. The doctor with that frog-like face had told her they might be hard to deal with, but nothing in particular really stood out to her as worrying.

At this rate, it didn't seem like she needed to accompany them anymore. Time to get back to her own job.

Yomikawa sighed and pulled her back off the door. "Message for you two. The nice lady needs to go to her job at Anti-Skill, so don't burn the place down while she's away, 'kay? Be good children and I'll bring you back a souvenir or two."

"Okaaay! replies Misaka replies Misaka, flinging large quantities of water with her superpowered water splashing attack."

Ignoring the response of "you little priiiiiiiick," Yomikawa picked up the big sports bag at her feet and left the hospital behind her.

There was a sharp glimmer in her eyes.

Her bag was heavy and filled with the regular Anti-Skill equipment.

After Yomikawa left and the two of them had expended all their precious bathwater resources in the war, they came to a peace treaty.

"This is bullshit. The water doesn't even come up to my lap anymore…"

"I can barely even splash anymore, says Misaka says Misaka, though tilting her head and wondering if maybe she could do something with it if she were clever enough?"

"Stop. Splashing. I'm freaking *wounded*, in case you forgot!!"

"Actually, your hair grew out crazy fast and stuff, so you can't even see the surgery scar anymore, says Misaka says Misaka, impressed. Wait, would it be against the rules to encourage regeneration of your body tissue from the electric signal vector level? asks Misaka asks Misaka, her eyes all glowy at the wondrous secrets of the human body."

"I'm telling you, the cracks in my skull haven't fully healed up yet!!"

"Splish-splash bubble-bubble kicky-kicky!"

"…"

"If Yomikawa knew how much bathwater we just wasted, she'd be angry, says Misaka says Misaka, shaking. But maybe she won't come back to the hospital today, suggests Misaka suggests Misaka optimistically."

"Eh? You've heard somethin' about it?"

"Weeell, not from Yomikawa, says Misaka says Misaka…"

CHAPTER 3

Light Hidden in the Wreckage
"Remnant"

1

Tokiwadai Middle School had two student dormitories: one within the Garden of Learning and the other without.

Kuroko Shirai and Mikoto Misaka roomed together in the one outside it.

"Kah…hah…?!"

Shirai had managed to drag herself to the dorm's back door, then very nearly coughed up a chunk of blood. Forcing down its aftertaste in her throat, she kept pushing ahead. She needed to do some first aid on herself as soon as she could, but her body wasn't moving the way she wanted it to. Given the pain she was in, she couldn't rely on teleportation, either, since its strength was volatile.

Her right shoulder, left side, right thigh, and right calf.

Those were the points stabbed by the sharp metal that had torn through her clothes' fabric, which was now forcibly thrusting into her wounds. With every step, she felt a strange stiffening feeling with her clothes and her skin, lending an odd sense to her pain.

Her flimsy bag felt like a barbell.

That drove home how much stamina she'd lost. A cold tremble settled into her stomach.

Having made it to the back of the dorm, Shirai looked at the line of windows and saw the lights in hers were off. *Thank goodness…Big Sister hasn't…come back…yet…*She smiled very thinly and concentrated her energy at her core.

There was no way she was walking in the front in tatters like this. Mustering a shredded formula out of her pain, shivering, and panic, she teleported directly into her own room.

For a moment, her body was weightless.

The sensation of crossing space felt closer to being thrown than gravity going away. It was like a roller coaster. A heavy tension gradually rose from her stomach.

"…Gah…"

Now safely on the floor of her dark room, she wandered to and fro unsteadily, not turning on a light, gathering her first-aid kit and a clean uniform. She cut down on the amount of work she had to do by a little bit by deciding to use the underwear she'd bought earlier that day. After unhooking the clasp on her bag, she took out the package from the lingerie shop.

With that in hand, Shirai opened the door to the bathroom and entered. There were no windows in there, so it was pitch-black. After closing the door, she fumbled for the light switch and flipped it. With a *click*, the white fluorescent lights filled the small bathroom.

"Ah…guh…"

The strength left her hands, and everything she'd carried in clattered to the hard floor. She tried to prop herself up on the wall, the dart piercing her side scraping it in the process. Body shivering as if it had been shocked with electricity, she lost her balance and collapsed to the floor, causing all sorts of other kinds of pain to tear through her.

Aug…ust…twenty…first…

She couldn't think straight with the pain. Still, as she sat on the floor, she tried. Had anything been odd on August 21st, like that woman said?

If I recall correctly...Big Sister didn't get home until pretty late... That was the day **that gentleman** *suddenly showed up at the student dorm...* Having gotten ahold of one thing, she began dredging up the rest of the information. *The gentleman was gone in a flash... Oh, that's right. The teddy bear under Big Sister's bed got dragged out, and then there was a strange windstorm blowing through the streets. I heard a train switchyard on the outskirts of Academy City had some sort of explosion, and people saw really bright lights...*

Finally, she remembered the rumors going around about that day. She looked up despite herself. *Unconfirmed information that Academy City's strongest Level Five got taken down by someone... Ugh.*

She'd heard the stories had been immediately covered up by the Academy City General Board to prevent useless disorder and unrest. Because of that, Shirai didn't know *who* exactly it was who had beaten the strongest Level Five in the city.

A giant explosion, flashing lights, and an M7-class windstorm. The switchyard thought to be where it happened looked like a bomb went off. Reconstruction work was being spearheaded by Anti-Skill, but Shirai had assisted them as a member of Judgment, too. At the time, everyone was saying the same thing.

The ravages of this destruction were not ordinary.

The Level Five who caused all of it was definitely the strongest in Academy City.

But...

How strong must the one who calmly stood up to a Level Five during such a catastrophic disaster be?

*And not only that...*Shirai had gotten wind of another bit of news on her own. *It's possible that Big Sister was present at the scene of the battle between the two espers.*

She'd seen it.

She'd seen all the switchyard's cargo containers destroyed, their contents strewn about. Many things of all kinds, shapes, and sizes were everywhere. Nobody would have stopped to think about a single coin on the ground—but Shirai did.

As soon as she picked it up, she knew.

It was the kind of cheap coin people used at arcades.

It was also the kind of coin a certain girl favored as bullets for her Railgun.

The intense pain interrupted her thoughts. It would certainly appear August 21st had been no ordinary day. But how much did that have to do with all this? She couldn't tell.

She came to the decision that treating her wounds came first.

She lightly touched the corkscrew in her right shoulder—the first attack she'd taken—with a finger. The sharp, thick, spiraling piece of metal would probably tear her muscles further if she tried to pull it out normally. Fortunately for her...

"My goodness...This ability sure is good to have at times like these."

She teleported it. The corkscrew in her shoulder vanished and reappeared in front of her. With nothing left to support it, it fell straight to the floor and made a clear ring.

Blood came from her shoulder. She'd uncorked her shoulder, letting the blood flow out. She hadn't taken the metal darts and such out of her wounds yet because she hadn't been prepared to immediately stop the bleeding until now.

She groaned as her world swayed, then shook her head to force it back into focus. Looking at the bloody corkscrew on the floor, she clicked her tongue. *A majolica porcelain grip on a Sheffield opener...No thought to where it was produced, its history, any traditions, any ideals—a stateless corkscrew. What an upstart I ran into.*

As she began teleporting the metal darts in her sides and legs in the same manner, she took out her cell phone with her empty hand and punched in Kazari Uiharu's number.

"Hello, this is Uiharu. Shirai, I looked into what you asked about...Whoa, um, you seem to be breathing in a lot of pain."

She'd actually given Uiharu a quick call before getting back to the dorm, explaining what had happened—how she'd lost and how the luggage was stolen again—then requested that she investigate the Tree Diagram, look into the identity of the teleport-type esper, and try and plot out a few possible escape routes she would have taken, though it would have been hard given the woman's ability.

She'd also told her to keep the fact that she was wounded on the down low. She knew that not doing so might have provoked a different obstruction for her.

Anti-Skill, led by faculty, went on the more important missions, not the student-led Judgment.

It was for two reasons: one, because they couldn't expose children to danger, and two, because they couldn't give children such overwhelming power over others.

With these major wounds, Academy City would have restricted her from doing anything else. But that teleport user had spoken of things that raised a lot of questions about Mikoto Misaka, Tokiwadai's ace, and things of that nature.

She didn't feel like turning in so easily.

"Are you really okay? Gung-ho women aren't in style right now, you know."

"Nobody...asked you. Did you find anything?"

Discarding the bloody darts on the floor, Shirai worked her tattered body and reached for her clothing. She removed her summer sweater, short-sleeve blouse, and skirt hooks, then groaned. The red had even gotten to her underwear, she realized, then took all that off and threw it on the floor, too. She hadn't taken off her leather shoes upon coming in, either, so she removed them, too, then her socks, then the leather, metal dart–holding belts around her thighs as well. Now stripped of all her clothes, she checked her wounds in more detail.

"About the teleport esper—the data banks say there're fifty-eight of them in Academy City, including you. Sure aren't many people who can work through special eleven-dimensional calculations, huh?"

"Anyone who…matched…my information?" She pulled a first-aid kit over to her with a bloody hand.

"There are nineteen espers who can move multiple objects at one time, again with you being one of them. And," continued Uiharu, "there were about three people who matched the description of the culprit you gave me. But only one of them doesn't have an alibi. The other two were spotted on cameras." Without seeming to be in too much of a hurry, Uiharu gave her conclusion. "Awaki Musujime, a second-year at Kirigaoka Girls' Academy. She uses a teleport-type ability like you, but it works a little differently."

"As…I found out…I mean, she took…ten men at once…and made them block for her! They must have weighed…around seven hundred kilograms in all. It's…way above…my power." She didn't deny her own weakness—as long as she believed there was a way out of this.

She flipped open the first-aid kit lid and took out a tube-shaped object. Closing the lid, she squeezed the tube, forcing gel onto her wounds. This was an emergency external-wound treatment kit with three effects: disinfecting the wound, stopping the bleeding, and preventing it from opening. Apparently some amazing medical scientist nicknamed Heaven Canceler made it, but it wasn't distributed to the public. You could close up most wounds with it, but it couldn't deal with minute, irregular situations. If this kit didn't work, it was time to see a doctor.

"Well, yes, but it's actually fundamentally different. Your teleportation lets you touch an object and send it to a distant place—you can send it from you to point A. But Musujime can move a distant object to another place—she can send an object at point A to point B. In her case, the point of origin isn't fixed."

"So that's why…That woman, she called herself a Move Point esper…" Shirai bit her lip and thought a little. She'd definitely been moving things all over the place without her hands touching them. But she had never tried to use her ability on Shirai's actual body. If she were able to do that, then she would have slammed her into a wall or something instead of using a roundabout means like using throwing weapons. That much was for certain.

"There's some interesting experimental data here. Apparently her power can't be used to teleport other espers with similar abilities. Since involuntary diffusion fields are still a budding topic of research, they don't know why, but apparently similar involuntary diffusion fields will get in the way of Musujime's ability… From what this report says, it specifies it doesn't only apply to Musujime but to any espers with teleportation abilities—they can't teleport others with the same type of power. Is that true, Shirai?"

"I don't know! This is the first time I've met someone else with teleportation." She sniffed. She'd never tried it before, but she could make a guess. Espers with teleportation moved around with their absolute coordinates in eleven dimensions in mind, not in three. Even if one tried to alter the spatial coordinates of another teleporter, that mental positioning system probably served to hinder the process like a wedge.

"And I have some boring old data, too. In her curriculum two years ago, Awaki Musujime's powers went crazy and she apparently got pretty badly hurt."

"…Yes, that surely *was* some boring data. Nothing about any of this suggests a weakness. Why is a monster like her only Level Four, anyway?" Chewing on that, she took some tissues out of the pocket of her torn skirt and started wiping up the blood clinging to her wounds. Her skin, oddly, was a little cold as she felt the gentle elasticity it gave in return to her pats.

"I'd think you could fight on even footing even if it was against an official Level Five anyway, depending on how you went about it. Maybe she's got a weak spot." Easy for her to say over the phone. "Anyway, about the Tree Diagram, well…"

"I want to believe it was just her rambling like a lunatic, but it must not be good from the sounds of it." Shirai began to wrap bandages over the gel that had coated her wounds. She could tell she was sweating a bit, and touching the cloth confirmed it.

"No. I searched for news reports about the Tree Diagram being destroyed, but I came up with no hits. They're saying it's still floating in satellite orbit, and they're saying the scheduled extra-vehicular maintenance for Academy City's shuttle that launched last month has nothing to do with it."

"What is going on, then?" Shirai frowned, stopping her work, then thought back to the single photograph she'd been shown as she lay in a heap in that alley. A photograph of a broken satellite.

Uiharu didn't sound convinced, either. "I suppose that's good news…? Another one of our teams captured the one they stole the luggage from, but he was just a courier. He said he had been told to do this by District 23 and didn't know anything about a satellite. We had a psychometer look into his memories, but they confirmed what he said."

A courier. *A professional one, maybe?* she thought. He seemed to be quite tenacious about his job, considering he tried to pursue the group of culprits even after they'd stolen his luggage… "So District 23 was trying to deliver the luggage's contents to some other research facility in Academy City. So they used a courier to transport it. And then, someone—probably Musujime's own group—snatched it away. The one it was snatched *from* wanted to take back the luggage, but he couldn't make a fuss about it because it was all supposed to be secret. That's why they needed to get it back themselves—is that it?" Shirai slowly moved her bandaged arms and legs to make sure no blood was still coming out. The quick-drying gel had hardened already, completely closing up the wounds.

"I wonder about what department District 23 was trying to deliver the luggage to in the first place, but investigating the robbers is probably more important. I think there's a chance an outside organization hostile to Academy City is working behind the scenes. You have an eyewitness account, and besides, if they were from Academy City, too, they wouldn't have relied on such a crude robbery."

"…An outside organization hostile to the city. Could Musujime be related to something like that? Just who is she?"

"She's been absent frequently from Kirigaoka Girls' Academy. And they're all excused absences, too. Which should never happen if she's not doing work for Judgment."

"Are you saying whatever work she's doing compares to ours?"

Uiharu's voice got smaller. "This isn't confirmed, but according to some, she's the guide. To the building with no windows or doors."

"…The Academy City General Board chairman's headquarters."

It was a very movie-like rumor—that the leader of Academy City lived in a special building that could even absorb and disperse an impact from a nuclear missile. It had no entrances or exits, no windows or doors, so apparently they needed to use a "guide" who could teleport in and out.

But if those rumors were true (or if it were more than that) then Musujime would be familiar with circumstances the general populace wasn't. It wouldn't be strange for her to be in contact with some special people. And maybe the outside organization thought that was important.

"I do not know what Musujime's circumstances are," said Shirai, "but I will consider that she was in contact with an outside organization and caused this incident. The contents of the luggage…She called it the 'remnant.' Now that she has it…"

"…All she has to do is bring it to the organization waiting outside the city and hand it off to them."

"Do you know what route she will take?" She reached for a change of underwear, but then noticed again that her hands had blood on them. She went to the sink instead and washed them. In a normal situation, she would have seemed like a dunce—a girl in pigtails washing her hands in the nude, cell phone between her face and shoulder.

"That one's tough. With teleportation, it wouldn't matter what route she took. You know as well as anyone that even Academy City's security systems have blind spots." She paused. "Oh, but if the security *would* catch her, that could actually give us a clue."

"What do you mean?" asked Shirai, wiping her hands off with a towel and putting her feet through her panties. She pulled them up to her waist in one go—a little too far, so she pushed them back down a bit with her fingers.

"If she's going to slip past the security systems, then we just have to check all the blind spots. Compared to all of Academy City, there's quite a bit less ground to cover, right?"

"…You say it like it's easy. I'm wounded, you know…Ow!" Right when she tried to hook her small brassiere around her back, a pain shot through her side. She must have caught her skin in it. Frowning at not having chosen a front-hook or a slip, she rubbed her side. Thankfully, it hadn't caused *another* wound to open.

"…" Kuroko Shirai very briefly gave her underwear a once-over. Mikoto Misaka had called her tastes bad, and she felt (fairly seriously) down about that. However, she didn't actually pay much attention to the underwear's actual design. Underwear wasn't for showing off—it was for wearing. She would take more comfortable underwear over the alternative any day. The fabric in underwear with childish designs on them sometimes felt thick and cheap, and it was distracting to have it rubbing against skin when she moved around. Seriously, if you were going to choose something like that, you might as well not be wearing anything under your skirt at all (though in her case, she needed to maintain her composure to use her abilities). She and Mikoto couldn't agree on this, and it made her disappointed.

Once she was finished putting on her underwear, she wrapped the leather belts she used as metal-dart holders to her thighs. She didn't have any spares. After rubbing disinfecting alcohol from the first-aid kit on the ones that had been stuck in her body, she packed them back into the belts.

"Umm, well, listen. If she was trying to get out of Academy City by crossing between blind spots starting at the scene, then including both underground and above ground, a number of routes are naturally available to her. So doing a thorough search would—"

"...Shh!" Shirai detected someone present and quickly hung up the phone. A moment later, she heard the sounds of someone coming into the room from beyond the thin bathroom door. Shooting a glance at the bathroom door, she realized she'd forgotten to lock it, and she hastily shut it and did so. The metallic *clink* echoed awfully unnaturally.

"?...Kuroko?"

There was no mistaking that voice. Even slightly muffled by the thin boards, she knew who it was right away. She would have only needed to hear her *breathe* to be confident it was Mikoto Misaka.

"What, are you taking a bath? You should at least turn the lights on when you come back here. It was pitch-black. What were you doing?"

Shirai gave a start. She couldn't let Mikoto see how wrecked she'd gotten. She mustn't even act in a way that would let her imagine what she looked like. The girl was far more the type to burden herself with the problems of others than she herself realized. "I-it's called conserving energy, Big Sister. Poor little Kuroko

was being kind and considerate, trying to slow global warming even a little bit."

"Uh-huh. You know, Academy City is mostly wind-powered. Carbon dioxide has nothing to do with it, does it? And it's supplemented by things that don't run on fuel, like solar power, too. I mean, using the air conditioner is another problem, but..."

"Oh, really? And here I just wanted an excuse to invite you into a nice, dimly lit atmosphere, Big Sister. —Oh, come, Big Sister, that kind of groaning is very improper for a lady." Shirai giggled, leaning against the door. The door vibrated; Mikoto must have done the same thing on the other side. As Shirai felt that, she remembered something.

*Didn't you think things were a little too convenient? Like how the useless person who stole this practically aimed to get wrapped up in a traffic jam? You couldn't guess the reason **behind the electricity failure on the traffic lights**? There's no possible way you wouldn't know what kind of powers Tokiwadai's ace has.*

—She knew something was happening.

Mikoto Misaka sure has it rough. Someone blew up the Tree Diagram for her, so her nightmare ended.

—And she knew Mikoto Misaka had a lot to do with it.

But now they're saying they're going to repair it. If that happens, they'll redo the experiment. So, well, I suppose I can sort of relate to her feeling she needs to struggle desperately against that.

—And she knew that even though Mikoto was wrapped up in these problems, she would never show a hint of distress or worry to Shirai—no, she didn't *want* to.

She knew. All she had to do was put together the pieces to understand. Mikoto had her own issues, but she didn't want to reveal them to Shirai, and someone else was responding to them. And whatever her reason may have been, she preferred Shirai to be that way...as if repelling her from some private circle.

If Shirai had done her best, had worked so hard she shed her own blood…

…then Mikoto Misaka would never be happy about it. Never. Because that meant Mikoto had gotten her wrapped up in her own private affairs.

But even still…

Shirai felt strongly that she wanted to do something for Mikoto. She wanted to lighten her load, even if she couldn't do much. Even if the things Shirai devoted herself to were never revealed and that credit was given to someone else—she didn't care. That's what she wished for. Staring at her bloodied clothing from inside her wound-covered body, she clenched her teeth and prayed for it.

Kuroko Shirai didn't know about any of the specifics.

She hadn't been told anything, so she couldn't make any judgments.

But she wanted to end it.

She wanted to make sure to take her out of the situation—of spilling her own blood for something.

And once she put an end to everything, she wanted them to be able to laugh together again without any background things to worry about, like they had today after school.

All alone, Kuroko Shirai made up her mind.

And to do that…*I will offer you serious lies, Big Sister, even if you don't want me to.* "Big Sister, where have you been?"

"Hmm? Grabbing one or two accessories I missed out on buying, I suppose. Recently I've been looking all over for them, but I just can't quite seem to find them. I just stopped back here to pick up something I forgot. I'll be going out for a bit again. Oh, but don't expect any souvenirs, Kuroko."

What a weak argument. Shirai wondered what she'd do if she said she would come along with her, like she always did. *Recently…That means Big Sister has been doing something by herself lately. Looking for accessories? Top-secret ones, perhaps…? Good grief, you said it.*

Shirai smiled thinly but didn't back down. There was one thing she needed to say. The thing Mikoto had told her this afternoon. She would turn the implication of those words right back on her. "Hopefully it will not rain tonight. The weather forecasts haven't been correct lately, after all."

"..." For a brief moment, Mikoto inhaled as if surprised. Then, after a few moments of silence, she spoke, her voice a little softer than before—as if tired by something. "You're right. Thanks for worrying about me. I'll do my best to come back as soon as I can."

She felt her leave the door. After pulling her back away from the thin boards, she seemed to exit the room. She heard the *bang* of the door to their room opening and closing.

"Anyway..." She took a breath, then, still in her underwear, snatched up her spare summer uniform and got her phone back out. There was something she needed to ask Uiharu. "Yes, that's right. Could you be a dear and tell me where that utter piece of trash could have gone?"

2

After cleaning the bloodstains in the bathroom and dealing with her torn clothing, Shirai teleported again and exited onto the road behind the girls' dormitory.

It was 8:30 PM.

Privately, she was a little surprised it hadn't even been two hours since going shopping with Mikoto.

At this hour, the transportation facilities of Academy City would be mostly shut down for the night. The bus and train operation schedules were all aligned with the end of the school day, one reason being to prevent kids from being out late. The only things on the roads would be the cars of faculty and university students, taxis, and other trucks for business purposes.

It seemed that the traffic had already cleared up.

Of course, there were very few wheeled vehicles in Academy City to begin with, so it made everything look smooth.

Shirai took a breath of air. Its smell and taste had already changed to that of the nighttime.

"Umm, I have some useful news, Shirai." Her cell phone was saying something. "It doesn't seem like Awaki Musujime is able to move her own body continuously like you do. There was a note about that in the data banks. Do you remember how I told you her abilities went crazy during a curriculum she took two years ago?"

"Yes, what about it?"

"After that, she frequently made use of the school counselors. I wonder if it could have traumatized her somehow. She hasn't gotten good results in experiments to make her own body move, and apparently she has a history of pushing herself so hard that her health breaks down. Like every time she moves her body, she has to summon all her courage to do it. Which means..."

"...That if she kept trying to warp herself, she'd get mentally exhausted in no time flat, is that it?" Shirai bit her lip a little. "I suppose I didn't see Musujime teleport her own body during that battle. If she could do that in the first place, it would have been faster for her to steal the luggage herself and run away than it would be to call in outside agents. We can move at high speeds, ignoring walls and roads—we don't need to limit ourselves to traditional means of pursuit."

Even Shirai's own abilities largely varied based on her mental state on a given day. Maybe Musujime's strength would plummet, too, if she dug up the girl's trauma during combat.

Still, though. *Is that why such a powerful esper is still stuck down here with me in terms of Level?*

With that bitter idea in mind, Shirai began to teleport. Every time she advanced eighty meters and set foot on the ground again, she'd immediately determine her next destination and warp there.

In honesty, her body was such a mess that she could barely walk. At times like these, the ability to freely move continuously at a high speed seemed quite reliable.

"In Musujime's case, she may be able to move things from far away, which I can't—but on the other hand, the calculations are that much more demanding. I can only move things I'm touching, but that means I don't have to calculate the coordinates of its original location."

"Yes...I suppose so. —You can...shrink the calculations...that way. Anyway—as for the predicted routes...Musujime could utilize without...using Move Point..."

Shirai paid close attention to the voice coming out of the phone, which was stuttering because of the side effects of teleportation, but before Uiharu had the time to finish, Shirai was given the proper directions by something else.

Boom!!
A thunder-like noise reverberated from somewhere far away.

Kuroko Shirai looked up at the night sky. "Could that have been...?"

Academy City's transportation facilities, store hours, and the like were all essentially made to match school hours. Lights faded quickly as the sun set, so compared to other urban centers, this one had less artificial lights. The view of a sky full of stars tonight meant it was clear out, which implied there were no thunderheads—nothing to make lightning strike.

Then where had the scream of high-voltage electricity originated?

"Shirai, we have reports of a large-scale battle between espers happening in District 7, Area 1. It's right on Musujime's predicted escape route!" To overshadow the volume of Uiharu's voice and to block the transmission of electromagnetic waves, thunder roared once again.

She knew for sure. There was no mistaking that tone color. "Big Sister!!" she shouted, changing course. While she felt carelessly exposing herself to Mikoto went against her style, when she imagined the girl being attacked by someone, she could no longer choose the option of staying put.

She used teleportation to move from point to point through space, one after another.

As she did, the sounds of seemingly violent sparks rang out like a bombing attack.

The men and women out, all older than Shirai, were looking that way dubiously, their night walks interrupted.

Shirai advanced on and on as though hurried by both of these things, discovering her destination was near at hand. She quit using her high-speed movement via continuous teleportation, moving toward the corner of the building—right where the blind spot was—from where she'd heard the immense sounds of electrical attacks.

As a detective might do when tailing a suspect, she poked her head around the side of the building to take a look.

And then she saw it.

3

It was a battlefield.

A battlefield created by a single girl.

Its location: a building under construction. Thinking back, it was the same place as the accident where the steel framework had collapsed on August 31st. They had removed the broken pieces of frame getting in the way and looked into strengthening the remaining sections already—and they had just begun to rebuild it...or so she recalled.

A minibus lay on its side in front of the building's entrance.

Its windows were broken and its contents were strewn, but nobody was inside it.

Everyone who had been riding it had dived for cover inside the building under construction, hoping the scattered mess of steel frames would give them some kind of barrier.

All in all, about thirty men and women were hiding in the building. Some were armed with guns, and others were Academy City espers.

Those guns! I remember them. They're the ones those guys I wrecked with the luggage were carrying...!!

Shirai sucked in her breath as she peeked out from the building's shadows. Both the guns' design and the way they held them were similar.

Nevertheless, Mikoto Misaka was just standing there next to the toppled bus.

I know who those people with the guns are. And that idiot woman said Big Sister was deeply involved with that luggage. Which means...

Given the format of all this, she could guess these were the guys trying to give the remnant to the outside organization.

Someone she knew was among them.

Awaki Musujime.

None could present an obstacle to Mikoto. There may have been a fallen minibus right there, but she wasn't trying to use it as a shield. Common sense would suggest how utterly defenseless she was when faced with dozens of enemies all with ranged weapons...

...but she easily crushed that common sense, showing them what the nickname Railgun really meant.

Light erupted from Mikoto Misaka's fingertips.

Her coin was launched at three times the speed of sound, easily slicing through the thick steel frames supporting the building. The men with the guns took a blast from the slight fragments, swept away just like that as the esper who'd been aiming at Mikoto's head from an upper story lost his footing on the crumbling supports and was swallowed down into it. The single Railgun had crushed through almost twenty steel frames, finally coming to a stop after inflicting cracks on the wall of a different building.

A few of the flustered men tried to withdraw farther inward, but Mikoto's electricity put a stop to that. Pale blue light flew from her bangs, striking a portion of the steel framework, then immediately ran through the entire building. Anyone touching the framework was instantly blown backward, and even those who weren't were sent to the ground, electricity piercing them from all sides as they tried to make their way deeper into the metal coffin.

There were a few espers who remained through a combination of luck and some factor or other, and those tried to rally. They were too late. The difference in their powers was too great. Railgun blew away an aeroshooter's vacuum blade after causing little more than a gust of wind. A telekinetic fired a handful of wooden stakes at her, but she flooded them with high-voltage electricity and they exploded. Even another electromaster had passed out from sheer terror before even using his power.

She was almighty.

This was no more than a hopeless battle, a demonstration of why Level Fives were called Superpowers here.

This was how different the abilities of the only seven in Academy City really were.

The fact that no one had died in this situation actually felt like a *joke* to Shirai. Unless she took into consideration her own attacks, her opponents' movements, and how the destroyed objects would move, she couldn't have such mercy. It had been an offhanded attack, and yet a mixed team of dozens of people was already in shambles.

Then, Shirai remembered when she'd gone back into her room after treating her wounds in the bathroom. The lid on the savings bank on the side table was off. The small treasure chest–themed container would have been filled with the arcade tokens she used as bullets for her Railgun.

Mikoto *still* hadn't taken a single step. All she did was gaze levelly at the finished battlefield and announce disdainfully, "Come out here, you coward. I'm not impressed at how you use your allies as a buffer."

"Would you like me to regale you with a sweet tale of not letting my friends' deaths be in vain?" The voice in return was still calm enough to reply. Dragging the big white luggage with one hand and actually smiling, Awaki Musujime appeared on the third floor atop some steel beams. The men, knocked unconscious by the high voltage, were scattered around her. She'd probably warped them to her the moment of the attack and used them as a literal shield. The flashlight dangled lazily from her right hand.

"Villains like you are all so petty. You seem elated. You didn't think escaping me for forty seconds meant you'd beaten the Railgun, did you?"

"Not at all. If you'd been playing for real, that attack would have reduced this entire area to rubbish. Perhaps that's why?" Musujime set the luggage down on the steel beam, then sat on top of it. "Still, you seem to be in quite the rush tonight. Usually you prefer information warfare. You've never brought the direct force of your Railgun in to disrupt the experiment, despite its power. Are you really that afraid of the remnants being put back together? Or is it about the reconstructed Tree Diagram being mass-produced internationally? Or, perhaps, that someone will restart the experiment before long?"

"...Shut up, you foul woman." Sparks leaped from Mikoto's bangs with a *crack*.

Still seated on the luggage, Musujime swung the flashlight up and down as if to beckon to her.

...

Shirai took a peek around the building again to confirm to herself that it was Musujime who Mikoto was facing down. She still didn't grasp what their connection was, but they were definitely in combat.

She thought back to the words Musujime had spoken. *You didn't know? Well, it doesn't seem like you're being used without knowing it...Tokiwadai's Railgun doesn't have that kind of character.*

*They're evidently not complete strangers...*Their conversation didn't seem at all like this was the first time they'd met. They'd probably clashed before, and now Shirai was getting a glimpse of a small piece of that.

Clashed? With Big Sister? And she's still at it?

Battles didn't need to be fought cleanly, of course. In fact, given Musujime's personality (not that she knew much of it), she seemed more the type to pull surprise attacks from the shadows.

But still, just being able to *stand* after fighting Railgun was abnormal.

She considered how to best make use of the current situation. She couldn't just saunter on out there; there was a marked difference in her and Musujime's skills. Besides, she absolutely wanted to avoid acting carelessly, messing up the battle, and causing Mikoto to get hurt because of it.

"Heh-heh. Why do you worry so much about weaklings? Besides, those things you seem to hold so dear were *created* for the experiment. It should be fine to destroy them. It was the original intention."

"Are you being serious right now?"

"Oh, come now. In the end, you're fighting me for *yourself,* aren't you? Well, so am I. Those who fight for themselves, with their own strength, in a way that suits them get other people hurt. What's wrong with that? It's stranger to be patient with something you hold in your hands. Right?" scoffed the one who had calmly used her allies' bodies as shields.

Saying that when all was said and done, she wielded her strength for her own satisfaction.

That they were the same, so one getting so violently angry at the other was strange.

Instead, Mikoto Misaka smiled a little. "Yeah." This time, pale blue sparks started crackling all over her body, not just from her bangs. "I'm pissed off. So pissed off it feels like I'm about to burst a blood vessel. Yes. Digging up the remnants of the Tree Diagram, idiots showing up to rob something for their own profit, trying to reignite the experiment everyone finally got around to settling. Yeah, that makes me angry. So angry I have half a mind to wage a digital war on the central players involved in all this and crush them all at once." The light in her eyes focused directly on Awaki Musujime. "But I'm even angrier than that right now."

Those words caused Shirai, who was thinking up a plan to help Mikoto—or at least, to not make things worse—to stop thinking.

"...That idiot. Did she think I wouldn't notice? She didn't sign in, the room was a mess, the first-aid kit was gone. Did she think I wouldn't realize what a terrible situation she was in just from hearing the pain in her voice from across that door...?"

Shirai nearly choked. *Now* she knew what she was mad about.

"That's what I'm mad about most of all. The fact that I got an underclassman wrapped up in all this. She did some slipshod first aid on herself instead of going to a doctor, and even beaten up like that, she still won't give up! To make things worse, she left you alone! Everything she told me just made me more worried!! I'm furious that my underclassman could be this stupid!!"

Shirai's chest tightened. Musujime wouldn't have understood

what she was saying. Plus, Tokiwadai's Railgun didn't know Shirai was here. So who was she shouting at?

She kept it a secret from Shirai. She had a transparent excuse all ready to go about looking for accessories. She warned her numerous times with that ambiguous advice that the weather might get bad. And now, she was all by herself. What had Mikoto Misaka been fighting for until just now, and in this place?

"Yeah, I'm mad as hell right now, and it's because I'm selfish! Mad at that unreasonably perfect underclassman, mad at the piece of trash who dared to hurt her, and, most of all, mad at myself for causing this horrible situation in the first place!!" Mikoto shouted as though she were driving a blade into her own chest. As if to put an end to both the Tree Diagram incident and to the person she was snarling at. "If you say this incident started with the experiment, then the responsibility lies with me. Responsibility for my idiot underclassman getting hurt and responsibility for you hurting my idiot underclassman! If everything is my fault, then I'll stop you, using every last bit of privilege and duty I have!!"

Shirai knew.

Why was Mikoto trying to fight Musujime alone, behind Shirai's back, when she was already fighting?

She was neither Shirai's ally nor Musujime's enemy.

She had chosen the path of stopping everybody here without going along with anyone.

All by herself.

She even pointed her metaphorical blade at whatever nightmare she was holding inside herself.

"I'm putting an end to this once and for all. There's no reason either one of you needs to be dragged along by the experiment—by that despair."

Crossing her legs on top of the luggage, Musujime giggled. "You're as kind as you are sentimental. It isn't as though you *created* the silicon-corundum unit. If you would just complain that you were a victim here, too, like normal people would, we wouldn't have to be fighting."

"You say that the reason you started this fight was because of our experiments. Whether that was the Level Six Shift experiment or the Radio Noise trials."

??? Level Six Shift? Radio Noise? They sounded like code to Shirai. What did they refer to?

Musujime, however, seemed to understand. "They were not *yours*—they belonged to the Sisters and the strongest of the espers, didn't they?...And I see you've wrested the story from the *allies* of mine you took down. About my reasons. As you're an esper yourself, then, you should understand—I cannot be caught here. No matter who I need to sacrifice, no matter what means I need to use, I will have you let me escape."

She got rid of her lighter tone with that last sentence, at least. Shirai readied herself from around the corner of the building. What was Musujime's maximum teleportation range?

Mikoto narrowed her eyes a little. "...You think you can run from my electricity with a measly Level Four ability?"

"Oh, my. I certainly wouldn't be able to avoid an attack at the speed of light after looking at it, but that's about all. If I just read your movements beforehand and warp in conjunction—"

"That won't work." Mikoto cut her off cleanly. "This isn't the first time we've fought, you know. I'm sure you've realized it yourself. There's a little hitch in your ability. You can move whatever objects you please, but you can't move your own body. I can understand that. If you warped somewhere dangerous, like inside a wall or into traffic, it would be all over. You don't care how many others get hurt so you can save yourself. You'd want to eliminate the unlikely possibility of destroying yourself, wouldn't you?"

"..."

"Why don't you say something? Did you think I wouldn't have noticed that by now? You use your Move Point on the bodies of allies and signboards and stuff as a distraction, but you still physically run away. Of *course* I'd see something wrong with that." Mikoto sighed, thinking it absurd. "Besides, anyone normal would have run away in such a disadvantageous situation. Or are you just unwilling to do that? Anyone could see you don't have any room to relax, here."

Awaki Musujime smiled thinly. But perhaps someone with good eyes would have noticed her fingertips trembling just slightly, but unnaturally.

"It's probably got something to do with that incident in the data banks where your powers went berserk. You don't hesitate to teleport other people or objects. It's only if you have to teleport yourself, isn't it? I bet you'd have to spend two or three seconds to make absolutely sure your calculations were correct." And then Mikoto said, "How many shots do you think I can fire in three seconds?"

"...Was there that much information in the data banks?"

"Don't make me answer that again. It doesn't all need to be written in the data banks for me to figure it out just based on your face and how you fight."

In response, Awaki Musujime's smile deepened. She brought her hanging legs onto the steel framework. Then, lifting herself off the luggage she was sitting on, she stood up elegantly. The languidly moving flashlight stopped. "But you see..."

—*If it's not my own body, then I won't hesitate to use Move Point on it.*

At her words, Musujime gathered almost ten people right in front of her. Each was one of the ones Mikoto had knocked unconscious with her attack. There were Academy City outsiders and espers alike. Adults and children. It was a literal human shield.

However...

"That shield...It's got a lot of holes!!"

Mikoto let sparks loose from her bangs anyway. Human bodies couldn't form a flat surface like metal plates could. If you got a bunch together, there would always be holes. She was going to penetrate through those slight gaps.

A lance of more than one billion volts of electricity. A moment before it fired out of Mikoto's hair, Musujime smiled from the other side of her shield. "A question for you." Her tone was cheerful, despite the situation. "How many unrelated people would you say are in this shield?"

What?! Mikoto immediately slammed on the brakes.

In her hesitation, the three-second delay came and went. A moment later, Awaki Musujime disappeared into thin air. With the luggage.

Every one of the unconscious people fluttered down toward the steel beams below. They were all people Mikoto had just taken down. Musujime hadn't used a single unrelated person in her shield.

"Damn it!!" she swore, looking around the area. She hadn't moved to anywhere in sight, of course. The annoying thing about teleportation was that it moved from one point to another, so there was no obvious line to her anyone could follow.

Shirai caught a glimpse of Mikoto's face for a second. She didn't appear to be looking at anyone. If she had been, she definitely wouldn't have let them see her about to cry as she was.

Kuroko Shirai rested her back against the wall, hid herself, and, glaring into the void, thought, *All right. It is now my turn, Big Sister.*

If she were in Musujime's shoes, where would the teleporter go in order to escape Mikoto Misaka's pursuit?

Plus, how much would she leave herself open in the relief of having escaped from the Railgun?

I do beg your pardon, Big Sister. Even if your idiot underclassman heard what you said and knew just how much you were worrying about her, my will to see this through has not bent even an inch. They would need a similar esper in order to go after her. Someone who *could* move freely, ignoring the flow of traffic and the thickness of walls.

"Okay, Kuroko Shirai, you can do this. Once more into the breach—and make sure to come back alive."

She placed her Judgment armband on the shoulder of her uniform.

A second later, after having reaffirmed her mission, she was gone.

INTERLUDE THREE

—I need to hurry.

In a pitch-black hospital room, with all the lights out, a certain girl rose from a bed.

—I must make haste, thinks Misaka, revising her priorities in their entirety.

She looked like Mikoto Misaka, but she wasn't. She was Little Misaka, serial number 10032, who had been created from Mikoto's genes.

Broadly speaking, she was an esper who could control electricity, and also a group of espers who communicated via electrical signals to anyone on the same brain wavelength. After a certain incident, she had been imposing on this hospital to get her body treated. Most of the other Sisters were using facilities outside Academy City. Units like Little Misaka who had remained in Academy City were in the minority.

What was internally spurring Little Misaka onward right now was information from the other Sisters of the same type who'd been sent to facilities around the world and the conclusion drawn.

by that serial number 20001, Last Order, who integrated and managed all that information.

She had been collecting fragmentary data from the rest of the world before now, but upon accumulating and unifying all of it, a huge problem emerged.

Misaka will reconfirm now, says Misaka 10032, initiating optimization of everyone's memory information via the network. She gave a look around her, then grabbed with her right hand the special goggles placed on the shelf near the bed. *The reason eight nations and nineteen organizations are presently launching or planning to launch shuttles under the pretext of space research and development is because they wish to retrieve the remnants of the Tree Diagram, conjectured to be in satellite orbit, correct? says Misaka, offering a question to the many units in the network.*

If that were true, then they wanted to rebuild the Tree Diagram.

That would be why incidents were springing up regarding the remnants necessary for that purpose.

Restoration of the world's most powerful parallel processing equipment equated to a resumption of the experiment. The very same one a certain boy and girl had risked it all to bring to an end.

Similar movements present in Seville, affirms Misaka 10854.

Rocket launch plans confirmed in Schleswig as well, reports Misaka 16770.

I have received information that Novoslbirsk has already collected part of the fragments, follows up Misaka 19999.

Still in Novoslbirsk, study results report that the core part necessary for restoration, the silicon-corundum unit, is in Academy City, and that the Tree Diagram cannot be completed with the other fragments alone, says Misaka 20000, offering supplemental explanation.

As Little Misaka sat up in bed and swung her feet to the floor, many voices, emotions, and images flowed directly into her head like an avalanche. They were the voices of her Sisters, who had been left in the care of agencies and organizations supporting Academy City across the world, and were now receiving treatment. By constructing a network using the brain waves of all the others, they could acquire information from 9,969 places in the world in a heartbeat.

Presently, the only remnant absolutely needed to restore the Tree Diagram must be in Academy City, speculates Misaka 10044.

Perhaps the fragments other agencies have acquired, as well as the pieces left currently in satellite orbit, are being ignored by Academy City simply because they cannot be used by themselves to restore it, further speculates Misaka 14002.

In the same vein, Cape Kennedy is currently advancing a plan to infiltrate Academy City to steal the remnant, reports Misaka 18820.

Apparently their group is called the Asociación de Cienia, adds Misaka adds Misaka and stuff. Oh? Should I have said Misaka 20001 instead? asks Misaka asks Misaka, wondering to herself.

Little Misaka clenched her teeth at the endless flood of opinions being sent.

None of it was good news.

The very act of her getting multiple confirmations on the answer was partially because she wished it were some sort of joke, but she didn't appear to realize that herself.

"It is already past the time Misaka is allowed out, but I cannot stay here, says Misaka, driving herself on with the excuse of urgency."

She placed her hands on her nightclothes. They weren't pajamas or a negligee but a simple surgical gown. She undid the string in the front, exposing her utterly naked white skin. She cast off the surgical gown as if dropping her bathrobe to the floor for a lover, then took a towel and simply wiped the sweat from her skin. She could feel through it that her body heat was slightly higher than normal. Her poor physical condition came with a slight fever. All of her skin, too, was tinged ever so slightly with redness.

With somewhat unsteady legs, she put on a pair of panties, reached behind her to hook on her bra, did up the buttons on her short-sleeve white blouse, pulled up the zipper on the side of her skirt, reached her head and hands through her summer sweater, then sat on the bed and put her socks on one at a time.

Then she put her goggles on her forehead and put on her shoes. Finally, she picked up the surgical gown off the floor, folded it, and placed it on her bed. The minimum required preparations had been completed in an extremely short time. She spared a glance for the door, but then shook her head and moved to the window, unlocking it and sliding it up.

She looked down. This was the second floor.

Little Misaka didn't pay any mind to that fact, though.

In any case, dealing with the remnant within Academy City is the top priority, concludes Misaka 10032. Yes, the Tree Diagram's restoration must be avoided, thinks Misaka, renewing her determination as she remembers that boy and girl. Misaka does not wish to bring a shadow over their faces.

Despite her determination, her expressionless eyes contained a hint of anguish.

The boy had run to the switchyard that night to save Little Misaka, who had been badly beaten.

He had shouted to her, ignoring even the likes of Academy City's strongest esper.

She remembered. She remembered what he had said.

"..."

She shook her slightly feverish, dazed head and set herself back to thinking about practical things.

The situation involved them, and it was advancing even now. They weren't at the epicenter of the incident, but by collecting information from places all over the planet's crust, they had successfully gotten a vague idea of what was happening.

And despite knowing all that...

...neither Little Misaka, nor any of the Sisters, could set foot into it.

There were less than ten of them, including her, still remaining in Academy City.

And most of them were receiving treatment for their excessive genetic manipulation and the side effects of their controlled growth acceleration. None of them were in a state to deal with an emergency—much less be used in combat.

Little Misaka knew.

She knew the name of the one who stood up for her when her life was in peril.

So once again, she decided to entrust their fate to that one boy.

To the boy who came all alone to the switchyard that night. To the boy who stood up to Academy City's strongest Level Five with nothing but his fist. To the boy who gritted his teeth and rose again, no matter how many times he fell or how many times he was attacked.

The first thing to come to her mind at a time like this was his face.

And his expression—unyielding, no matter what the situation.

Of course, she didn't want to get him involved.

But she had no one else she could rely on.

She was powerless.

She bit her lip a little at her own inability to do anything about her problem herself. That, combined with the fact that she was getting someone else wrapped up in a big problem she couldn't solve herself.

Even still, she, or rather they, didn't realize.

That the anguish they were feeling now was their heart, which had never needed to feel something like that until now. Nor that the anguish was the other side of the same coin—the kindness of taking others into consideration.

The Sisters knew exactly where a certain student dormitory was. Little Misaka had acquired the information from carrying cans of juice there in the past. And now, out of all the Sisters currently in Academy City, she was closest to that position. Serial number 20001, also known as Last Order, was in this hospital as well, but being an incomplete specimen, she couldn't expect any physical abilities from her.

She placed a foot on the opened window frame.

I will confirm one last time, asserts Misaka 10032. In accordance with Plan 228, all Sisters in Academy City will each move to retrieve the remnant.

Number 10032, you have received an especially severe amount of physical damage compared to the others, so should you not devote yourself to your treatment? asks Misaka 10774, showing her concern.

As the voice reached her mind, Little Misaka's body wavered slightly.

The Sisters were somatic-cell clones who originally had short life spans. Various things had been done to them in order to construct a physical body in an even shorter amount of time. They were undergoing treatment to regain the balance this had caused them to lose.

Even among them, though, Little Misaka's current weakness was above all the other Sisters because of the persistent attacks from Accelerator during the experiment. Walking around the hospital for short periods of time was one thing, but even Heaven Canceler couldn't give her permission to engage in genuine activity on the level of real-time combat.

Her body was still suffering from a slight fever. Her sense of balance swayed a little, and it felt like the floor got squishy.

For now, that was everything.

If she forced herself to do more than a fixed amount of exercise, her fever would immediately grow much worse. She would even be in danger of coughing up blood and collapsing as a result.

It does not matter, answers Misaka 10032, she declared despite all that, gazing unflinchingly into the darkness out the window. *What are these wounds compared to the situation? asks Misaka 10032 in return. Misaka will not stand and wait until she fulfills her promise to that boy, repeats Misaka 10032 in full understanding.*

For just a few seconds, she stopped receiving information from the network.

Eventually, like a wave coming back toward the shore…

Acknowledged; we will entrust this to you, says Misaka 14458 with a nod.

We will leave this to you, agrees Misaka 19002.

*Misaka will rely on you, too, says Misaka says Misaka. Wait, Misaka wants to do something, too; she can't stand doing nothing, and **he** hasn't even come back yet from wherever he went, says Misaka says Misaka, waving her hands and feet around.*

Little Misaka frowned slightly, then said, *Misaka 20001, your role in Plan 228 is to remain where you are and act as an information processing relay, advises Misaka 10032. Also, aside from that, who is "he" exactly? asks…Misaka 20001. Please respond, declares Misaka 10032, though it does not look like she will get an answer.*

Serial number 20001, Last Order, had apparently severed the connection after saying whatever she wanted, and she didn't answer Little Misaka's call. *Troubling*, she thought briefly. Last Order was originally created as a host specimen who could send an emergency stop request if the Sisters were to go berserk, so the Sisters couldn't give Last Order commands or restrict her actions over the network.

In any case, Misaka will move on her own, says Misaka 10032, disconnecting.

She jumped out of the window without a mind to her skirt. Her summer Tokiwadai Middle School uniform fluttered in the night breeze. At the moment she landed, she folded her legs under her to soften the impact. She had originally been programmed to turn aside the recoil from firing anti-tank rifles in combat. A fall of a few inches wouldn't damage her in the slightest. Of course, she wouldn't be able to do the practical calculations fast enough if it were something she hadn't predicted beforehand—like sudden combat damage.

She shot off at full speed, breaking out of the hospital grounds. She jumped a fence, dashed into the road, then began immediately shortening the distance by using the labyrinthine array of back alleys.

Even while she ran, she was sweating. If she had been more emotionally abundant, she would have thought the sweat was icky. She was currently receiving treatment from the doctor with the face quite similar to a frog's—and she was in a much weaker condition than the other Sisters because of her fight with Accelerator.

But she ran on anyway.

If the information of serial number 20001, Last Order, was correct, if the remnant were retrieved, the Tree Diagram restored using it, then mass-produced, there was a risk that the experiment would be resumed as a result. That one fact they had calculated indicated a danger to the lives of all the almost ten thousand living Sisters.

A risk—and a danger.

Still running at full speed, Little Misaka wondered to herself how she had come to be able to make judgments like that.

"Misaka now has a reason she cannot allow herself to easily die, concludes Misaka. Generally speaking, I'll pass on dying, thank you very much, declares Misaka."

Yes—she made a promise to that boy.

She needed treatment. When it was all over, she'd be with him again.

It was a comforting promise.

And one that would be very painful if she broke it.

Little Misaka reached a main street from an alley, then dove into another back street. She knocked over a garbage can, sending a wandering stray cat frantically running away. She narrowed her eyes painfully, but there was no time to apologize.

There was only one person she could rely on when situations like this happened.

It wasn't her logic saying that, but rather her experience.

So now that she had felt herself to be in danger, she was trying to tell that to a certain boy.

"Still...," said Little Misaka into the empty air. If she asked him for help, it would mean sending that boy into a battlefield yet again. At the same time, though, she knew that even if she avoided getting him involved and kept quiet, then if and when the experiment was started again, he would go charging in, no questions asked.

Yes—she could say for sure.

He would come no matter what.

If the experiment did get resumed, if the Sisters began to be killed off according to a plan again, then he would clench his fist, not even thinking about how much of a risk it would be to intervene.

"If he would get involved whatever the case, then it would be safer to tell him before the situation worsens, concludes Misaka. Of course, it would be best that nobody got involved in Misaka's problems, but Misaka does not seem to have the right to such lip service, given how she has left this to someone else already, says Misaka, her shoulders sagging as she continues her all-out sprint."

She got out onto a large road, then skidded on her heels and turned. She began to run faster as she weaved through the waves of people.

That moment.

Crack! came an ache in her temples.

...!

Her head was spinning. White noise had come across the electrical network comprised of the Sisters' brain waves, which was something that almost never happened. As Little Misaka sent a message to the network warning them that something strange had occurred, she sharpened her senses to search for a cause, bringing the goggles on her forehead down to her eyes.

Electromagnetic wave interference due to super-high voltage electrical current...Perhaps the Original could output this sort of power, speculates Misaka without any evidence. I can estimate the location to be within five hundred meters, but...

Such an immense high-tension current would have no use other than battle. Little Misaka was worried about that, but heading for the student dormitory came first. She put her goggles back on her forehead and ran farther.

A second later, she arrived at the dorm's entrance.

Diving into the elevator, she pushed the button for the seventh floor, then as the elevator slowly ascended, she went over in her mind how to parse and reduce the information she needed to tell that boy. Whatever the case, time was of the essence. She needed to convey correct information to him as quickly as possible, while also conveying the sense of danger she felt from the situation.

She wondered if he'd listen to her if she barged in at this late hour. She wanted to know the exact time, but she didn't have a watch. Sending a signal out to the network, she immediately received various times at places around the world from the other Sisters. Combining them and recalculating led her to the current time in JST.

The elevator made an electronic noise.

Its doors opened with a shaky, uncertain clatter. Little Misaka immediately resumed her all-out dash. The entrance to her destination was the one door that had had its railing rebuilt recently for some reason.

Coming to an abrupt stop in front of the door, she politely rang the intercom, then turned the doorknob a moment later anyway, not caring what he thought of it. The knob turned with an insecure lack of resistance. Perhaps, for those living here, it actually wasn't late enough that she would be considered rude, concluded Little Misaka vaguely to herself, throwing open the door.

Touma Kamijou was inside.

The girl named Index was inside with him.

They were both in pajamas, and for some reason the girl had climbed up the boy's back and had her teeth in his head. A cat, perhaps reacting on instinct upon seeing the female devourer, was trembling alone in a corner. Surprised at the sound of the door opening, they looked at Little Misaka at the entrance.

She considered.

What sentence would change his mood the fastest in this situation?

Logic gave up on answering that, and experience guided her instead.

She spoke.

"I have a request, says Misaka, looking straight at you and speaking her mind."

As she spoke, she wondered what had changed about her to allow her to say that.

"Please save the lives of Misaka and Misaka's Sisters, says Misaka, bowing to you."

The boy didn't have any questions.

He just prompted her to continue.

CHAPTER 4
Those Who Settle the Score
Break_or_Crash?

1

As Mikoto Misaka searched for her, Awaki Musujime stood beside a window with a white rolling suitcase next to her, and looked down at the other girl from above.

Awaki Musujime was inside a building. The fourth floor of this one in particular belonged to a pizzeria. Not a delivery place or a fast food restaurant, but a real one that served pizza for its menu. Given the cheapest single thing available cost over 3,000 yen, it wasn't a place meant for middle school kids. The establishment catered mainly to university students and faculty, so even now that it was approaching nine in the evening, it showed no signs of closing up for the night.

There were many fancy tables with brand-new tablecloths on them, and although it took away the silence from the restaurant, the French pop music playing through the cable radio was soft enough that it wouldn't get in the way of people having conversations. The tables filling the room didn't even cover half of it, but a sign saying CLOSED was already posted at the entrance. The moderate amount of space between the seats was part of how the place created its atmosphere.

Despite people seeing the Move Point esper suddenly appear

from nothingness, chaos didn't ensue inside the restaurant. Perhaps they were long since aware that this was just that kind of city.

Using their consideration to her advantage, she continued to look down. She could see Mikoto look about, then go into one of the narrower roads somewhere.

Phew... Finally, she knew relief—she could breathe again.

No amount of straight-line distance would help her against Tokiwadai Middle School's ace. Unlike her Railgun, which slowed due to air resistance at a certain range, her electric attacks went at the speed of light. They would reduce any distance to zero in the blink of an eye.

—It didn't matter how close she was; she only had to flee into Mikoto's blind spot.

—And she needed to be able to see Mikoto Misaka losing track of her from a safe location.

Those were the two major conditions. Thus, for her location, she had chosen "up." From here, she could watch her enemy go past and think up a way to escape at her own leisure.

Urgh...!!

As soon as relief came over her, she was overcome with a violent urge to vomit—an urge she'd forgotten about until now.

The burning stomach acid caused pain in her throat. Barely managing to return the contents of her stomach to where they belonged, she appeared, on the surface, to avoid any further difficulties. Sweat had formed in the hand gripping the military-grade flashlight.

In the past, Awaki Musujime had lost a handle on her control over her ability, Move Point, and ended up in an accident. Because of that, whenever she tried to move her own body with it, she felt immense tension and fear, enough to negatively affect her physical condition.

Therefore, she wanted to avoid teleporting her own body as much as she could.

Damn it. Maybe it's unavoidable, but why is it so terrible?

Thinking on it, she didn't like guiding VIPs into the windowless building at that person's command, either. Just sending someone to the other side of a wall was one thing, but especially the part where she had to Move Point along with the important people, not even the smallest failure would be allowed. On top of that, there were a few people who didn't seem anything like VIP material mixed in: like a blond high school kid with sunglasses and a red-haired priest.

She placed the luggage on its side and sat down, then wiped off the sweat forming on her brow with a handkerchief. It certainly was nerve-racking jumping into a building you couldn't see inside. Warping into an oven would get her roasted, and coming out over a ventilation shaft would mean she'd fall a moment later. You could snort and say that wouldn't happen normally, but just the fact that cases like this were *at all possible* was plenty scary enough.

In any case, Mikoto Misaka had completely lost Musujime's trail. Normal people confined themselves to actual roads to look for someone. That meant if she warped from the top of one building to another, people on the ground would probably be blind to her. Her maximum teleportation distance was over eight hundred meters. Unfortunately, she wasn't confident that she could keep her body moving continuously. If she warped four times, the contents of her stomach would spurt out of her mouth, her senses would be confused, and she might not be able to keep using her ability in that state.

From a mental health perspective, the most she would use Move Point on her own body was once or twice. For now, that meant completely escaping pursuit with just that, then running on foot for the rest of it. Her plans were starting to coalesce—

Dpshh!
There was a high-end corkscrew stuck in her right shoulder.

"Agh...?!" She knew that corkscrew. It was the one she'd stabbed the Judgment girl with just a few hours ago. When she really considered what that meant, a familiar voice came to her from behind.

"I'm returning this. It hasn't even a scintilla of taste, after all. People don't want to see things like that. Oh, and these, too."

Right as she said "too"—

Gsh-dbsh-gshh!! Sounds like things thrusting into a mud-soaked cloth repeated. Her side, her thigh, and her calf. She knew all too well why the metal darts were stabbing into those particular locations.

The searing pain surged through her, converged in her brain, and exploded.

"Hah...gah..."

Awaki Musujime turned back into the restaurant from the window. The patrons looked confused, startled, and generally at a loss for what to do at the sudden occurrence.

Among them was only one who didn't.

A girl was sitting on one of the fancy tablecloths on a table, grinning confidently.

The restaurant seemed too high-class for its own good.

Just like when Musujime had come in, nobody particularly seemed to care when Shirai teleported there.

"There's no rush. I missed your vitals...Quite easy to understand, isn't it? I pierced all the places you stabbed me. Oh, and that reminds me."

Shirai theatrically reached into one of her pockets. Musujime was immediately alert, but what she brought out wasn't a weapon. It was the tube of blood coagulant from her Judgment first-aid kit.

She flicked it from her fingers. It landed on the floor at Musujime's feet.

The girl with the twin tails grinned an evil grin.

"Use as much as you like. Please, remove your clothing, including your underwear; crawl around on the floor like a worm; and

tend to your wounds. Then, and only then, can you say we're even, you piece of shit."

Maybe they had considered the hostility in her words, or maybe they were afraid they might be included in the vilification themselves; the dumbfounded patrons and staff finally and suddenly rose and stormed for the exit. Tables and chairs were overthrown in the very *un*classy atmosphere, and with a tempest of footsteps, the restaurant emptied in no time.

Now it was just the two of them, staring each other down.

The distance between them was around ten meters. Teleportation and Move Point. It was within the effective range of both; at this point the concept of distance held no meaning.

Only the faint noise of the air-conditioning and the relaxing French pop music broadcast could be heard, sounding oh-so-innocent.

Shirai was sitting on a table.

It didn't appear to be due to composure. It secretly showed that her wounds weren't even letting her hold up her own body as she liked. Still, Musujime was in the same situation. Both had attacked the exact same spots with the exact same weapons. All one of them needed to do to guess at the damage done to the other was to imagine her own.

"…Now you've…done it. But…I suppose…I can't bring myself to hate…such a childish reprisal."

Musujime was sitting on the luggage by the window. She was forcing herself to appear relaxed—either as a combat bluff or because her pride was making her.

Whichever the case, neither of them was going to have a very easy time walking around.

But each of them had an alternate means of moving around.

"Well, this isn't very good," said Shirai with a smirk. "If they make too much of a fuss, my sagacious and impulsive big sister will come running straight here."

"‼"

"Your personality would never let you run from someone you could beat without doing anything, would it? No, I'd thought your methodology involved a lot of inflicting a lot of pointless wounds and feeling superior about it, then leaving, like you did with me."

Come to think of it, not once did Musujime attack Mikoto during their fight at the building under construction. Staying on the defensive and never launching a counterattack was proof she knew that she'd never be able to hold up in a square fight.

That meant that as soon as Mikoto Misaka arrived here, Musujime would lose.

The wound-covered Shirai didn't need to strain herself to beat Musujime. If she bought enough time for Mikoto to get here, she could get a second victory.

Musujime acted brave even when presented with that truth. "Hah. You seem to be pretty worried about Tokiwadai's ace. But even the Railgun isn't all perfect. Take Academy City's number-one strongest esper—she'd die for sure against *him*."

"Oh, I wasn't under the impression that either of *us* could reach that place anyway—the Level Five world." Shirai smirked. She spoke her self-defeating words with pride—as though it were proof that she really was worried about Mikoto Misaka.

Musujime couldn't help but scowl and click her tongue. *Is that why she made all the noise...? Not only did she pull a surprise attack on me, she created another victory condition by letting that Railgun know where she was...! In that case...* She started thinking immediately. What would decide her own victory wasn't whether she could take down the Judgment officer in front of her. It was whether Railgun chased her down or not. If she decided not to deal with Kuroko Shirai, and used Move Point to escape immediately—

"It will not work," declared Shirai, interrupting her thoughts. "You can't get away for good. I'm sure you know that! You and I are very much alike, you know. In this situation, with these wounds, in this place, with our abilities, with Big Sister following us...So what will you do? Do you think an esper with the same ability as you would be unable to predict where you would be going?"

"?!...You...You little...?!"

She lost it. She lost her cool so much that she couldn't put more than two words together. Shirai smiled very thinly at her. "Come, now, do you think I would be bluffing? If you do, then please, abandon that optimistic thought right this instant. I have prior information from the data banks. I have experience from crossing blades with you before. Plus, I have a similar mental structure as an esper with the same ability. My gut instincts have already given me quite a few pieces of supplemental information."

It was at that moment when Musujime finally figured it out. What was the meaning of all the actions Kuroko Shirai had taken up until now? *She stabbed me in the same places with the corkscrew and the darts...**to put me into the same situation as her?!** She was making my movement patterns easier to predict by compensating a little bit for the difference between us!*

They had similar abilities, similar handicaps, and similar thoughts—Shirai was trying to read ahead of time how Awaki Musujime would move. *I can't let this stupid girl do this*, she thought, gritting her teeth. She could use Move Point to get out of here, but her destination would be exposed for certain. She couldn't even be relieved if she warped to the other side of the world. There was no way. With just one teleport, her stomach hurt so much, it felt like it was being strangled. She couldn't stand it. She had finally prepared herself for death and used Move Point on herself, and this stupid girl could nullify that as many times as she wanted. Three or four teleports in succession were the absolute limit of her body anyway. She didn't want to waste her precious warps. Which meant...

"Yes, you have just one means of victory: to crush me before Big Sister arrives," she announced with an air of composure. "I, however, have two. Either I defeat you directly or I wait until Big Sister appears...Please, must I declare which of us is in the dominant position?"

That in itself *was* the declaration, and Musujime found herself surprised. She felt like the choices she'd had were being narrowed down, picked off one at a time. She shuddered—but then shook her head.

No.

She figured it out.

This Judgment officer wasn't making room for Railgun to intervene.

If she wanted to get her involved, she would have teleported her here right along with her.

Musujime smiled a bit. Once she figured that out, all sorts of other facts followed in its wake. Perhaps knowing her opponent's thoughts had backfired on her attempt to set up those artificial conditions.

Her mind cooled, and she began to regain her calm. "I swear... What a strange twist of fate has brought us together. Let me get this straight—you gave up not one but *two* chances to win?"

"..."

"The first chance was not bringing Railgun here. And the second was this attack. If you weren't so hell-bent on making this a game, you would have just killed me by crushing my brain or my heart or something. If all that really was for those cute ramblings of your Railgun, then you really are a sad person."

After she'd asked the question, Shirai's body had shaken a little.

Musujime knew why. She had the same sorts of wounds, after all. The damage they caused was severe. Plus, Shirai had been chasing her like that for hours now. Simply closing up the wounds wouldn't be enough to replenish her lost stamina. She was more exhausted than Musujime was. Musujime had just been injured now, but Shirai had been running with those injuries, so they had a different amount of stamina.

So she smiled—at her own dominant position and at the recklessness of her opponent. "How pathetic. You could have just compromised on your second hope. Why bother trying to go for your first one? Is your life really worth putting in that much danger?" she asked, still seated on the luggage.

"To protect the world that Railgun selfishly thinks is real…"

Kuroko Shirai looked back at Awaki Musujime's face. There was a strong, forceful light in her eyes, despite the fact that she was sitting on the table because her legs couldn't hold her up and her arms were dangling at her sides without energy. Both those things made it very clear how few options she had, but she wasn't making a false show of courage. She was just staring straight into the eyes of her enemy.

Even if it made her look stupid, she answered without hesitation.

"…I want to protect it."

To make matters worse, she was running on fumes—and she was pouring the last of her energy into this.

"Why wouldn't I…want to protect it? Of course I do. She may be selfish, and she may not ever spare a thought for our circumstances, but Big Sister wishes for something: a situation where neither you nor I would have to do any of this. It's so selfish and stupid, isn't it? She…Big Sister really believes she can settle everything just by getting everyone together, punching them in the face, and lecturing us. Even now that everything has gone to heck in a handbasket. I am actually considering trying to save you, even after everything you've done!"

Shirai smiled. It wasn't a mean one, just a normal one. "Big Sister is the kind of person who could look at this situation and say she didn't want us to fight, that she would appreciate it if we stopped trying to kill each other. There is no way Big Sister would feel nothing after imagining what I must look like now. She could blow you to pieces in five seconds if she felt like it—and that's exactly why she doesn't. She hopes there's some other way. Even though she could end things instantly with a coin and the flick of a thumb, even after all this, all she does is hope she can work things out and bear by herself all the pointless suffering that brings."

"…"

"Did you think Kuroko Shirai would refuse such a ludicrously infantile wish? By catching you by surprise and digging out your brains with a metal dart?! By bringing this to a swift end steeped in death and fresh blood?! All for my own self-preservation?! Do you think I am so unrefined I would get mud all over a doormat someone else laid out for me?!"

As Shirai shouted, she slowly lifted herself from the table. Her legs trembled but were firm. She was declaring that now was when things got serious. "I will grant you a return to your normal life. Just as someone, somewhere, wanted, and just as I've agreed with them."

"Then if I betrayed that, I suppose I would win," answered Awaki Musujime, still sitting on the luggage. She was declaring that she didn't want to go along with any of that.

2

It is so simple in the end, thought Shirai. Both she and Musujime were in very bad shape from their injuries. Even though she'd closed up the wounds, her stamina wouldn't return immediately. Just one shot—yes, just one light blow to tip over the opponent would be the end of it. With as many stabbing wounds as Shirai had, just ending up on the floor could potentially make them open back up.

If this turns into an all-out battle...I'd have about ten seconds at best.

She didn't need to be hit by an attack—just moving her limbs with all her energy would make her cuts open up. Nor did she have much stamina left in the first place. Losing any more blood would immediately put her into an unconscious state.

Musujime's power was overwhelming. If not for the condition stating teleport espers couldn't be moved with teleportation abilities, she'd probably just have warped Shirai into a wall or the ground and been done with it.

They stared each other down.

Ten meters between them.

Commotion could be heard outside the window.

There was one ringing sound, as though part of the framework of the building Mikoto had recklessly fired upon had collapsed.

And that was their signal to start.

Shirai brought her fist down on the table she'd been sitting on. With the sensation of ripping flesh, it shattered a plate. Grabbing the sharp pieces, she set up her teleportation. The ability made every attack sure to kill—she just needed to cut out of her target from the inside. Defense was impossible even by creating a wall, since the ability sent an object straight from one point to another.

In the same moment, Musujime activated Move Point.

Matching the movement of her flashlight, a silver tray shot toward Shirai, trying to hit her directly. It may have only been a tray, but a direct attack from Move Point could easily penetrate skin. It would be no less than instant death if it hit.

Shirai, however, moved before that.

She warped her body but a footstep's length to the side. The silver tray guillotine materialized in empty air and clattered to the ground.

Musujime had vast power, but she had the habit of swinging her flashlight whenever she triggered it, perhaps to get the timing right. Shirai would have a hard time taking the opportunity to launch a counterattack, since it ran the risk of a mutual death, but it made evasion a nonissue.

"Damn." Musujime frowned a bit. At the flick of her flashlight, five or six tables around them vanished and reappeared in front of her. They stacked atop themselves and fanned out, forming a giant shield that concealed her body.

She messed up...? thought Shirai. *No, that isn't possible! They're to conceal the fact she's moving out of the way...!!* She'd fallen for this trick once already. Coordinate attacks sent things from point to point, so the slightest differential in the target's coordinates would cause the attack to miss. Musujime had built a wall so that she wouldn't know she'd moved herself. *In that case!!*

Shirai teleported.

With the plate shards in her hands, she moved her entire body to a targeted location.

After she landed on the other side of the wall of tables, she prepared the plate shards again. *Correcting aim!*

If the wall obstructed her vision, she only had to jump to the other side of it. Then she would recalculate her target's coordinates, letting her accurately warp the plate shards to Musujime's location.

Awaki Musujime couldn't use Move Point on her own body at the drop of a hat.

Shirai lined up her shot, hoping for a quick conclusion...

Whoosh.

She heard something whipping through the air.

Musujime was standing just a step away from her. She had the heavy luggage handle in both hands and was twisting her body to try and bash Shirai in the face with the centrifugal force. With both her hands full, she held her flashlight in her mouth.

She could see it in the girl's face—she'd predicted Shirai would do this.

She looks relieved her extra insurance paid off...!!

With the corner of the luggage quickly approaching, Shirai teleported the sharp pieces in her hand to coordinates where they would sever the squared handle on the luggage.

The luggage flew in a different direction. Musujime's hands, now holding only the handle, swung around, with surprise on her face.

Now's my...chance!! Shirai poured all of her energy into her wounded right arm and tightened her little hand into a fist. It would be faster just to punch her at this range than it would be to go through the calculations for her ability.

Unfortunately...

Musujime jutted out her jaw a little bit, the flashlight still in her mouth.

"!!" Shirai was alarmed, but her thoughts couldn't go fast enough to activate her ability in response to Musujime's unexpected action. She immediately took a step back and watched as one color filled her vision. White. The color of the luggage, she realized, stunned. Musujime had called the flung-away luggage back to Shirai—without depleting its momentum, just correcting its direction to end up in her face.

If she hadn't taken a step back, the newly appeared luggage might have consumed her head. But, having evaded it, the heavy, fully materialized case flew at her face with force.

She'd realized it too late.

There was a loud *thud* as the heavy strike hit her. She bent over backward at the impact; she couldn't keep herself from falling.

Her skin all tightened up, and she felt something warm bursting from the wounds on her shoulder and side. Her fist flailed, hitting nothing. Opposing her will to endure it, her feet flew out from under her.

Just as she lost her balance, Shirai teleported.

Her body vanished, then reappeared, still about to fall over, but this time behind Musujime. She used her falling momentum to whip her elbow around and slam her in the back with it. Musujime shot toward the pile of tables in front of her. Shirai hit the floor before seeing that happen, and the impact this time didn't fail to reopen all of her wounds.

Guh...agh...!!

She rallied the last of her strength and grabbed something nearby on the floor to end things. It was the severed luggage handle. Sharpness was irrelevant for Shirai's teleportation attacks. *This...is where it ends!!* she shouted to herself, setting up the targeting equations at the same time to warp the handle she held.

...?!

But she couldn't use her power.

The weapon in her hands didn't move a bit.

The intense pain and panic had shattered her concentration, preventing the activation of her ability.

"N-no...!!" The fact made her panic even more. If only the pain got in the way of *her* ability, too, she hoped optimistically, looking over at Awaki Musujime.

But what she heard was another *whoosh*. And what she saw was the pile of tables Musujime had been shoved into disappearing. And also that she'd pulled the flashlight out of her mouth like a kebab.

Shirai felt a chill and shuddered. She immediately tried to roll out of the way, but above her, gravity pulled all those tables down at her like rain.

"...!!"

Still lying on her face, she set her hands on the back of her head to protect it. The heavy, blunt attacks showered her, striking flesh, resounding inside her wounds. She couldn't even writhe in pain with all the weight coming down on her.

Her narrowing field of vision showed Musujime, still down, kicking off the floor to avoid falling victim to the same rain of tables Shirai had. The darts piercing Musujime opened her wounds farther, and she screamed. Still, though, she used Move Point to get the handleless luggage back over to her, then, leaning against it, looked to Shirai.

Slowly, slowly, Musujime ran the tip of her flashlight over a nearby chair.

"Shirai, if you don't dodge, you'll die," she said with a broad grin. She dragged her flashlight over the chair and, like an airplane coming off a runway, thrust its rounded edge straight in Shirai's direction.

"!!" Shirai paled, but it wasn't like she could use Teleport anymore.

A chair appeared right next to the trembling Shirai via Move Point. It crushed a table, bringing the pile of them covering her tumbling down like a pyramid of playing cards. But it had only changed its shape—it was still preventing her from moving.

"Hmm. Considering you didn't move even then, it would seem you really can't draw up the teleportation calculations." The tension in Musujime's face began to loosen.

Then she laughed.

Despite the scattered blood from her open wounds hitting her cheek, she laughed.

She continued on, her tone jovial. "Hey, Shirai. Kuroko Shirai. Have you heard this story? Sheesh, I hear all sorts of things being close to *them*." Musujime checked where the metal darts and corkscrew were stabbing her, and then, with a deep breath and the swing of her flashlight, each one of them vanished and reappeared in front of her face. The darts and corkscrew succumbed to gravity and clanked to the floor. "A long time ago, there was a powerful esper who ran into a certain organization."

Musujime stood and backed up. Treating the wounds causing her pain seemed to be her top priority. She looked around, glancing here and there, searching for anything she could use as first aid. The tube of coagulant Shirai threw at her was on the floor, but Musujime kicked it away out of pride.

She's going...to treat herself...here...? And expose herself to me? I mean, she can't discard the possibility that Big Sister is headed this way... Shirai was dubious, but Musujime's expression looked rather relaxed.

Having taken the darts out of her body, fresh blood spurted from her wounds. Still, the smile on her face remained. That was gruesome in its own way. "The organization wanted to gain great power by somehow acquiring more of those powerful yet rare espers. So they decided to try and clone the esper. Do you know what the result of it was?"

Kuroko Shirai couldn't move. She managed to stick a hand out of a gap between tables, but flailing it wouldn't let her move the tables or attack her enemy. Musujime seemed quite satisfied at this as she tore a piece off the end of her skirt and wrapped it around a wound on her thigh.

Mikoto Misaka hadn't come yet. With how loud the battle was and how many guests and employees they'd chased out of the place, she would have surely noticed. Had she just not heard it? Or had she decided it wasn't related to the remnant? Shirai didn't want to call her here, but Mikoto's absence was quite a worry in and of itself. Shirai didn't think it the case, but perhaps there were still a few people from Musujime's group slowing her down.

But there was something stranger than all that. *Why does... Musujime look so relaxed...? She cannot possibly think she could win against Big Sister like that...*

In contrast to her dubiousness, Musujime spoke like she had a good bit of leeway. "It went terribly. The poor lambs they created didn't even have one percent of the original's power. Even one percent is enough to be used in the real world, but even with ten or twenty thousand of them in a group, they couldn't hold a candle to the powerful esper."

Soaked with blood, Musujime tore more fabric from her skirt and wrapped it around the cut on her calf. Shirai decided, without really knowing, that she'd wounded Musujime's pride enough that she unconsciously felt the need to tell a long-winded story to secure a more decisive victory.

Musujime's skirt was already short, and now her underwear was exposed; she gave a thin smile anyway. "You know, Shirai. Children made through cloning technology have the exact same genetics. Even their brains are constructed exactly like the original. So then why is there such a difference in their abilities?"

Her voice was brimming with overconfidence. It made Shirai want to barf, but if she kept ignoring her, Musujime would immediately lose interest and run away somewhere. With the luggage. "Wh-what a stupid…piece of fiction. Are you not aware of how Academy City's schools are assigned rankings…?"

The way abilities came into their own depended on the way a person was raised, even if they were the same person. That fact gave birth to all sorts of ability development theories, and the schools themselves started to be ranked with monikers such as "excellent" and "elite."

Musujime didn't seem to be particularly aggravated. "Oh, no. Each created individual was artificially put through the same talent-blooming process the original had gone through. And still, they couldn't catch up to the result they wanted. If the same brain didn't produce the same result, then don't you think there's something other than simple brain construction that relates to how abilities work? And if we could find those other things, wouldn't that mean we could give processing units that weren't human brains abilities? What I'm asking is..." Disregarding her own blood flying to her cheek, abruptly stopping her first aid, she said:

"Does the manifestation of abilities even *need* a human brain?"

Shirai gasped.

Ideas based on quantum theory were deeply involved in development of abilities in Academy City. The abilities conducted measurement and analysis of reality using purposely distorted processing and decision-making dubbed a "personal reality." Then, depending on the results, they would achieve the creation of some phenomenon by unnaturally altering the probabilities of the infinitesimally microscopic world.

"What...are you talking about?" But Shirai still couldn't help asking the question. "The curricula in Academy City...They're the culmination of *brain research*, aren't they?"

"Well, yes, but you see...The processing for all these phenomena— the observation and analysis of a target, I mean—do you even need to be human to do it?" she asked, seeming delighted. "For example, even plants can measure light. Some leaves and flowers close up at night. Can you say those kinds of plants *aren't* measuring the world?"

Musujime tried to close the wound on her shoulder, but her skirt was already an unusable mess. Instead, she removed the winter blazer she wore over her shoulders, tore off a piece of the long sleeve, and used it as a bandage.

This isn't good, thought Shirai. Once Musujime finished her stopgap treatment, she'd do something. But the only means Shirai had of hoping to hamper whatever that something was was to attack with her words. "Th-that's absurd. Do you even hear yourself talking? If *reacting* to light is all you needed, then you're saying photographs and posters faded by ultraviolet light can observe the world. The basis of abilities is what to *do* with that information. That's why Academy City goes through the whole personal reality business, which is different for everyone. What's special isn't our five senses, it's our ability to process things."

Musujime didn't show much emotion at those words, either. She took the belt her flashlight had been on and tried to wrap up the last wound on her side with it. Unfortunately, the thick belt made of metal plates didn't allow that. Instead, she removed the bandage-shaped pink fabric around her chest and wrapped that around her side. Despite them being the same sex, Musujime didn't appear to have any misgivings about exposing her breasts to a complete stranger. The most she felt was a little bit of apology as she swept up her winter blazer with the torn sleeve to hide her naked chest. "You're saying you can't use abilities without a high degree of mental activity?"

"Yes," answered Shirai, though she felt a discomposure in her heart. She knew she was being led on. The lack of argument from Musujime proved it.

"Then what about ants? They move in groups, using mass psychology to manufacture colonies and secure food. They receive honey from other organisms called aphids, and they repel ladybugs—it's a simple symbiotic relationship. A primitive form of reasoning, if you will…If you think their mental structure is irregular, then you're denying the way people think who are basically the same as you. They just have a minor difference in level," declared Musujime, making sure the cloth on her wound wouldn't loosen.

"You're just splitting hairs now…"

"Splitting hairs? Even they have a society with labor divided according to physical structure—king ants, queen ants, worker ants. Are you trying to discard their signal-based communication abilities that use their antennae or bioluminescent organs depending on the species, as well? If you are, then what exactly does a *humanlike high degree of mental activity* mean? Even insects have ethics and morals. Parent ants will protect their own eggs just like the rest of us." Awaki Musujime smiled very, very, very thinly. "Even ants can measure phenomena." She paused. "Them and us. Is it up to you to decide which of us perceives these phenomena correctly? How can you say for sure they would never be able to use abilities?"

Kuroko Shirai felt a chill go down her whole body. A single shiver, threatening denial of her very foundation as an esper. She looked at the thing Awaki Musujime was leaning on.

"Don't you think there could be plenty of things that are as good or better than humans? If it doesn't seem that way to you, then perhaps it is human hubris." Musujime smiled slowly, then stroked the luggage with a fingertip. "If you just changed your perspective slightly, you might learn how close such a thing really is. Yes, how extremely close it is."

The surface of the luggage gleamed sharply with reflected light.

The remnant.

The silicon-corundum processing core.

The Tree Diagram.

An artificial brain more efficient than humans', larger than humans', more complex than humans'...and yet slightly less flexible.

"Kuroko Shirai, you know how we sometimes say things have a mind of their own? If you're so stuck in your opinion that humans reign supreme, then I must say I'm a little disappointed in you."

Measurement of nature even ants were capable of.

Supernatural abilities that could manifest as long as one had a "mind."

If a human wasn't absolutely required for it...

...then, then that, would...

Kuroko Shirai stared at the luggage Awaki Musujime was

leaning against. "You…can't be serious. Are you saying abilities like ours have manifested deep down in that titan? Do you *seriously* think that? That's nonsense—you're claiming machines have *minds*."

But still.

But still, Shirai began to wonder. Was the efficient system called the "human mind" really necessary just to observe and analyze reality in the first place?

Musujime still didn't get angry. "Well, yes. That might be going too far. Machines are just machines, after all. Even if we took an AI that could adjust for camera shake and light exposure for a digital camera, for example, and presented it with some phenomenon, all the processing chip would be able to do is arrange the pixels of optical information on a screen. Data processing goes in an entirely different direction than the measurement of phenomenon in the first place." Her face actually looked relaxed. "In addition, it's true that no forms of animal or plant life capable of using abilities have been discovered, either. We don't actually know whether such a thing exists, but…" She brushed the luggage again. "If we have this, we can predict it. Using the ultimate simulation machine, capable of perfectly reproducing any phenomenon, would show anything and everything: the possibility of such creatures existing in our world and the progress of evolution of creatures ten thousand years from now. That is why I will assemble this remnant and acquire the Tree Diagram. Then I will ask it for every possibility under the sun—about whether any individual thing could ever use abilities in place of a human."

There was a strange light in her eyes. *That light is called delusion*, thought Shirai. "So that's why…you contacted an outside organization…?"

"Yes. The remnant may be valuable on its own, but I can't repair it by myself. I needed a group with the technical skills, the knowledge, and this particular objective." Awaki Musujime smiled.

Shirai found it difficult to believe that organization was wallowing in Musujime's ideas. They probably had an objective of their own. Plenty of people would want the Tree Diagram if they saw its specs.

"Shirai, what did it feel like when you first gained that ability?"

Shirai couldn't move, but she could sure as hell talk. From underneath the tables, she replied as if the answer were obvious. "Wh-who cares? The adults in the room got pretty excited about it, but as the person who got the ability, it wasn't surprising. It was just normal to me."

"That's right." Musujime paused. "I was honestly pretty scared," she said as though recalling events in her childhood. "I was afraid of what I could do with this ability. And when my fears were confirmed, it got even more frightening. You have to know something, Shirai. I was more scared of what I had gained than anything else in the world. I could *kill* someone with so much as a silly thought." At the moment, the girl no longer trembled over the past. "But I didn't have a choice in the matter. Only we have these powers. They'll be researched and analyzed in some lab we'll never see and go on to be useful to the world. That's why I *had* to keep this power. Somehow I managed to endure it, and yet…"

Musujime smiled—her grin slowly cutting across her face like melted ice cream.

"If I'm not the only one with this power, then I wouldn't have ever needed to have it in the first place. Hypothetically, if the user didn't need to be human, then why do they give powers to humans? If it didn't need to be me, then why did they give it to me? Shirai, you stopped thinking about it, believing it was natural. Leaving those adults aside, the other esper children with me before thought the same way, you know. They used the unfinished building as a shield, but they were the ones who first proposed this. Before they lost consciousness, I smiled and just told them to leave it to me."

"…" Shirai frequently heard stories about Level Zero children who couldn't get a power no matter how hard they tried turning into delinquents and gangsters. But this was the same thing. Even for those who happened to gain powerful abilities, some wouldn't be able to get used to it. Supernatural abilities were like the giant monsters in movies. If you wanted to live with others, you had to always be walking on your tiptoes, always meticulously careful. If you took a big, free step, buildings would be destroyed. In fact, being able to go all-out with powers on the level of Railgun was more unusual. They lived a life demanding constant self-control against outside pressure. In a way, they were essentially bound in handcuffs and shackles.

"Don't you want to know? Did we really have to gain these powers? Don't you want to know for sure if there was a good reason or not?"

Musujime spread her hands gently—as though she were beckoning to Shirai.

"You're no exception, are you? You've hurt someone with your own ability before. And you must have wondered why you had to come into such powers."

As if to embrace her—as if to suck her in.

As if she hadn't finished Shirai off yet because she wanted to say this.

"But I understand. You're like me. When you close your eyes, you think about how you've hurt others. And that's why…"

As if she were singing. As if she were whispering into the ear of a loved one.

As if Musujime had no real intention of killing Kuroko Shirai in the first place.

"I understand your pain. More than anyone. And because of that, I know how to acquire a method to take it away. How about it, Shirai? I invite you to learn the truth with me."

Her expression betrayed how she'd wanted to go on such a

long-winded tirade, despite running the risk of Mikoto Misaka arriving.

Maybe what Musujime said was something every esper would have to question.

As someone who had fought in this city with supernatural abilities, there was something she would have had to consider.

How skillfully could she hurt an opponent with her power?

How much damage could she do with it?

Would it hurt? Would they suffer? Could it break them? Could it stop them? Could it mow them down? Could it send them flying?

And after all of that was over, she would feel a sudden chill.

Why *did* she have something like this?

So she spoke out.

Did that chill back then really have to happen to her?

Why don't I contact an outside organization and rebuild the Tree Diagram to find the answers?

Shirai gritted her teeth.

The reason she was given her power.

The reason it may have been fine for her *not* to have been given it.

She felt some kind of foundation she'd created to support her mind waver, and said:

"I'm going to have to refuse that proposition."

Crushed under a pile of tables though she was, she cast a sharp glare at Musujime and spoke with a low, intimidating voice.

"I was wondering what kind of bombastic remarks you'd make after causing this much trouble. I am pretty disappointed. Big Sister *does* always claim how petty villains are."

"What…was that…?"

"Oh, please, don't get so surprised over something so obvious. Did you think your drunken logic would win Kuroko Shirai over to your side? You've seemed so relaxed this whole time. You weren't under the impression I would sympathize with you, then convince Big Sister on top of that, were you? Oh, or could it be that you just wanted to feel my cold eyes on you and shudder?

"Besides," she added, "animals? Evolution? Possibilities? Hah! You think they are important? Let's say you did some selective breeding on little tiny ants and got one to have an esper ability. How would that change *anything* for us?"

"Don't you understand? If other things were able to be given supernatural abilities, we wouldn't have had to turn into teleporting esper monsters! And if we didn't have to have such dangerous abilities, then—"

"Utter nonsense, if I may be so bold. I was asking you, regardless of what the possibilities are *now*, how it would change those of us who are *already espers*."

"..."

"If you had been pursuing the possibility for future generations, then I may have been simply moved to tears. But what will come of presenting a different possibility to those of us who have already become espers?

"And besides," she prefaced, firmly grabbing the floor with the hand poking out of the tables, "saying that espers hurt people is already evidence of a sore loser. If I had your power, I would help fix bridges or something, not stopping until the broken bridge was fully repaired. I would escort people trapped in the underground mall up to the surface. If you want to exert your powers to your heart's content, then go right ahead. Just so long as you do not misuse them."

With a creak, the pile of tables shook slightly. Kuroko Shirai gritted her teeth, trying to rally all the strength left in her wound-covered body, and said, "From my point of view, gibberish and sophistry are too good to call what you're saying. You're scared of power? You don't want it because you'll hurt someone?

That's what your mouth is saying, but which one of us is the idiot injuring people like this?! If you want to know whether what you're doing is right or not, then look at my wounds! They're your answer!!"

The many tables crushing the girl swayed and lolled. Her feet dug into the floor. She strained every muscle in her body for strength, despite the blood flowing from her wounds.

"Do you honestly believe that having a dangerous power will make people think you're dangerous? Have you ever thought seriously about how great power comes with great responsibility? You, madam, are an idiot! Don't you dare think Big Sister or I got where we are today with such ease!! We all put a lot of time and effort into thinking as hard as we can about what we can do with our powers before acting! Only after we acknowledged that did we create a place for ourselves today!!"

The mountain of tables wobbled and shook violently. Kuroko Shirai turned up the power, trying to fling away the heavy pressure coming down on her.

"Take a look at how Big Sister is running around outside if you like! If she felt like going all-out with her Railgun, she could settle this paltry problem in a minute! The only reason she discarded the simplest option is because she doesn't want it to end with a bloody tragedy!! She's putting herself in danger because of it!! I want to help her because I'm her ally, but even you, her enemy, are stupid enough to seriously feel like you want to save her, too! That is exactly why I call her my big sister!!"

The wobbling and creaking changed into a deafening clatter.

It started to fall.

All that weight holding her down started to fall.

"All you're really saying is that you're an esper with a special talent and everyone else is just part of the mediocre masses—running away with your dirty, high-and-mighty mind-set exposed! I will now proceed to beat some sense into those rotten guts of yours.

Once someone so mediocre beats you, you'll be forced to admit how mediocre you are! And I will send you straight back to the mediocre masses you came from!!"

Kuroko Shirai stood up.

Her clothes and body were sticky with the flowing blood from her opened wounds. She offhandedly grabbed a tall floor lamp nearby and held it at her side. Her hands dangling down couldn't use teleportation anymore.

But...

So what? said she.

I will beat you regardless of our abilities, said her expression.

Silently, she declared that she wouldn't be defeating her enemy because she had an amazing skill...

...but that she was standing up to her with a more powerful reason.

Kuroko Shirai inched along.

Forward.

One step, two steps, three.

All she did was wobble along, unable to maintain her balance, unable to even bring the lamp up in front of her, dragging it behind her instead.

And yet her vigor forced Musujime to move back.

A tiny yelp escaped her lips.

Shirai was strong.

Fundamentally strong in a completely different way, regardless of whether she had an ability or not.

Awaki Musujime's body, the blazer with one torn sleeve held to her chest, fell backward and tried to retreat. She could have moved more efficiently by using her Move Point, but she had *forgotten* about it. She couldn't set up the calculations amid all her panic and fear. Her eyes were no longer looking at reality—only the slowly walking image of Kuroko Shirai.

—I will lose.

Awaki Musujime had no grounds for thinking that.

—I will lose. It's not logic. It's absolute. I will lose.

Kuroko Shirai had already arrived in front of her. Musujime looked up, still sitting on the floor, and saw Shirai looking down at *her* instead with a glare.

Shirai's hand slowly rose.

She held the lamp like a baseball bat, lifting it unsteadily above her twin tails.

It was a great weapon.

Musujime may have been a Move Point user, but she only had the body of a high school student.

There was a faint *clunk*.

Before she realized it, the flashlight in her hands had dropped to the ground.

I will lose, she thought.

Awaki Musujime, the Move Point esper, could never win against Kuroko Shirai the teleport esper.

However.

However.

However.

Upon further thought, there might have been one thing Kuroko Shirai should have been cautious about from the beginning.

Just because Musujime was an esper didn't mean her power was her only weapon.

She might have caught on to this as soon as Shirai knew Musujime had contacted those men from the outside organization.

Cooperating with them meant it was possible they'd given her a weapon.

A deafening *thud* rang out.

Kuroko Shirai, the floor lamp raised high above her head—in other words, with her whole body exposed—slowly looked down at her waist.

A dark red hole had opened in the gut of her uniform, and a strangely colored liquid was dripping from it. A moment later, the window behind her displaying the night view of the city shattered into tiny pieces.

With the air conditioner's effectiveness dampened, the warm night air came inside.

Shirai's body tilted backward.

It seemed like the lamp's weight had gotten the better of her as she collapsed straight to the floor.

"Hah..." Awaki Musujime laughed, her right hand trembling hard. White smoke billowed up from the pistol her hand was holding. "Ha-ha..."

She had managed to take down Kuroko Shirai as she came for her.

But at the same time, Musujime was forced to admit one thing.

It had nothing to do with their abilities.

Until now, she had thought the fact that she was hurting people was a natural side effect of her monstrous power. But it had nothing to do with Move Point. Awaki Musujime was capable of hurting people even without her ability. The evil one, in the end, wasn't her ability—but *her.*

The evil one, in the end...

Musujime's lips dried. Her tongue dried. Her throat dried. She had tried to say that out loud, but her voice didn't come out. So instead, she delivered her conclusion in wordless silence.

The root cause of everything.

The one who had been hurting others nearby.

The source of the red color scattering around before her.

It was her own weakness—for finding solace by telling herself it was her unfortunate ability's fault.

Awaki Musujime thought back.

Back to the espers who had believed in the same thing she had. Her allies, afraid of their own terrible powers, fighting to search for whether or not they really needed to have them. The people who had begged her to use them as shields in order to protect her from Mikoto Misaka's lightning attacks.

Musujime believed that she was the same as them.

But her belief was different from the answer she'd found.

She...

...had stood with them only through deceiving them.

Even if she used the remnant to acquire the Tree Diagram, even if she investigated the possibility of powers nobody knew existed, everything had gone exactly according to Musujime's plan.

The most basic part of her would never be changed again.

The part of her capable of hurting others—it would be with her forever.

"Hah, ah...ah, gah. Gaaaaaaaaaaaaaaaaaahhhhhhhhhhhhhhhh-hhhhhhhhhhhhhhhhhhhhh?!"

She cradled her head in her hands, bent over backward, and let out a scream.

She had flung away the blazer she was holding, not aware of the trivial fact that her top half was naked and exposed.

With her index finger still on the handgun's trigger, even though she could accidentally fire it again—she tore at her own head, unaware even of such a simple prospect. She shouted and roared, her face muscles twisting and distorting, as if to eject everything pent up in the bottom of her stomach.

Bang!! came a deafening roar.

As Musujime sat on the floor, tearing at her hair, in her violence she had accidentally pulled the trigger. It happened to be pointing upward, and sparks flew from its muzzle, launching a lead bullet toward the ceiling. It bounced off, without piercing through, then struck the flashlight on the floor, bending it in half and sending it flying. However, she didn't bother to look at something so minor.

"Gah, ah!! Ah, ah, ah, aaaaaaaaaaaaaaahhhhhhhhhhhhhhhhhh-hhhhhhhhhhhhhhhhhhhhhhh!!"

Musujime, her face distorted like a beast, pointed her gun at Shirai.

But though she pulled the trigger, she didn't feel the recoil from the internal springs so peculiar to firing a gun. Only an empty *click* of pulling air remained in her fingers.

"Uuh, ah. Ah, ah?"

Musujime's head twisted.

Glancing at her right hand revealed only that it was in the shape of holding a gun—the actual *gun* wasn't there.

There was a soft *clank* from far away.

The handgun suddenly dropped to the floor fifteen meters to her side.

Move Point.

Of course, Awaki Musujime hadn't been trying to warp her handgun. It had flown from her hand on its own, without her thinking about it. It only took her a moment's thought to know why.

And that moment, her ability went off spontaneously.

There was a loud *roar!!*

Everything within five meters of Musujime—chairs, tables, forks, knives, decorative plants, menus, paper napkins, dishes, luggage—was blown away. All the objects crossed through space and warped outside in a neat circle with her at its center. As those tables and chairs in the circle warped right above her, there were many more loud bangs as they crushed other objects they teleported into. Teleportation didn't work on other espers who used that type of ability. Without that rule, Shirai might have been blown above the circle as well.

"..."

Musujime, oddly expressionless, pulled her index finger lightly.

The handgun returned to her hand in that moment, but there was a spoon caught through the middle of the barrel. It seemed like after she'd teleported the handgun, she'd teleported a spoon right onto it. Even an amateur could tell it was no longer usable.

She looked up to see all the objects above her in the circle repeatedly moving and warping like a tempest. The process overlaid object with object, crushed some and destroyed others, then fed their fragments back into the storm.

In any case, if she couldn't use it, she couldn't use it. She angrily threw the gun to the side without setting the safety. *Brrrack!* The gun ruptured from the inside, flinging pieces everywhere, but Musujime was no longer paying attention to it.

The circular tempest surrounding Musujime suddenly stopped.

The objects and fragments continually teleporting around her all ground to a halt and fell to the floor at once.

"I'll kill you…"

A low, twisted, distorted voice.

Sweat gathered on Musujime's chest like fat sizzling, being fried off a piece of meat.

"I will kill you! You, you!! How dare you break me like this!! If it wasn't for you, I would have still gotten through this!!"

Shirai, collapsed on the floor, smiled weakly at the absurd excuse. Musujime crawled over on top of her with a face of pure rage, perhaps having decided to strangle her.

But suddenly, she looked back up. "Hah. Ah-ha-ha!! How disappointing, Shirai!" She could hear Anti-Skill police car sirens from afar—they had noticed the commotion. "None of this *I'll take care of you next time* business. I will kill you no matter what. I can put an end to you somewhere far away, wherever I like. Because I am superior, and you're no more than a failure."

Musujime clicked her tongue and wobbled to her feet. "…The developers say any more than one thousand kilograms puts a strain on my body, but with Move Point I can teleport up to

4,520 kilograms. I can drive you into here even while running away. You *and* the whole building will crumble down to the ground." She spoke in a low, low voice. "Heh-heh, I'll break it all for you. You broke me, so I need to repay the favor, Shirai. I'll crush this entire building under you. I wonder how badly that will mangle your body?"

There was no reply to Musujime's voice. Shirai was looking up at the ceiling as if already dead. Musujime spat on the floor. Then, looking around, she picked up the blazer with the torn-off sleeve, slung it around her back, then located the luggage with the broken handle—

"Oh…I'm sorry, did you still need that?"

"!" Musujime turned around to the voice to find Kuroko Shirai laughing. Despite all her cuts, bruises, and wounds, her lips turned up in sarcasm, as if to say they weren't enough to stop her.

Musujime kicked Shirai in the side as hard as she could. She didn't stay to watch the blood spurting from the girl; instead, she grabbed the luggage, eyes bloodshot. With her objective and her methodology no longer aligned, she even ignored the consequences and the future.

Her face still bent out of shape, Awaki Musujime vanished into thin air along with the luggage.

Kuroko Shirai, however, couldn't use Teleport anymore.

If she stayed here like this, she'd be hit with Musujime's attack that was soon to come.

Maximum weight of 4,520 kilograms.

Apparently, using her full power harmed her own body, but in exchange, she could crush both Shirai and the floor under her. And it wouldn't stop there. If she destroyed the floor, then the entire building was sure to collapse like a failed block-tower game.

She had to get away.

Anyone else would have come to the same conclusion, but Shirai couldn't move even a fingertip.

Big...Sis...ter...
Her lips delivered a silent voice into the void.
She was far too distant for her feelings to reach.

3

It was a disaster inside the restaurant. The giant windows had been smashed, the neatly lined tables had been dragged away and turned over, the menus had been trampled under the feet of the fleeing patrons, the dishes and silverware lay broken on the floor, blood was scattered all over, and to top it all off, there was a girl covered in wounds on the floor. There were no patrons or employees. The very white light and the out-of-place French pop music drifting from the speakers were the only things controlling the room. The air conditioner couldn't keep up with its job at all now that the windows were broken.

"...Ugh..."

Kuroko Shirai, lying on the floor covered in blood, willed strength into her fingertips. Very slightly, they moved. But that was all. Her arms wouldn't move. Her legs wouldn't move. She couldn't get up, nor could she walk out of here. She couldn't even use her arms to crawl away. Plus, with how hazy her mind felt, she couldn't use teleportation.

This is the end of the road, she thought.

Awaki Musujime had already fled from here. But she probably hadn't gotten too far away. Direct distance or time didn't mean much when you were fleeing using Move Point. The question was how well she could cover her tracks by using the special privilege to ignore the flow of traffic and the thickness of walls she had.

On top of that, Musujime habitually felt terrified at the thought of warping her own body. She would be choosing her destination points very, very carefully so she could keep her number of jumps to a minimum. So at the moment, she would be hiding in a safe spot, constructing a route with which she would remain absolutely, positively safe.

And she had announced that she would kill Shirai for sure. That she would crush to death the dying girl by making use of her 4,520-kilogram maximum power.

Shirai didn't know when it would be coming. It could be five seconds, or it could be five minutes. She didn't think it would be five hours or five days, though.

Whichever the case, unless she got out of here, she was done for. *This is...the worst...* Her bloodstained hair stuck to her cheek and got into her mouth. *A tragedy...is what this is. Leaving the enemy alive, waiting for my own execution, and not only stupidly making her more excited but sending her powers out of control. How many people will Kuroko Shirai need to apologize to, to be forgiven for this?*

One girl immediately came to mind at the top of the list of those she had to apologize to.

Mikoto Misaka.

They weren't bound by any circumstances in their past—they weren't childhood friends, nor did their families spend time with one another. Shirai had met her after entering Tokiwadai Middle School...so since this April, and there wasn't some special agreement between them. At first, they really were just coincidentally attending the same school and happened to see each other in the same building from time to time.

But that was all it took to teach Shirai. Even if they only ever saw each other around school, it was far more than enough.

All the things Shirai were taught were simple.

Courtesy—it wasn't something you wore on yourself, but something to let the other person be at ease.

Etiquette—it wasn't something you forced on the other person, but a way to guide others.

Knowledge—it wasn't something to flaunt, but something with which to listen to the problems of others.

Pride—it wasn't for yourself, but rather first gained when protecting others.

It wasn't as though Shirai had been given a rambling lecture on the subject.

All she needed to do was *see*.

Being treated like that, whether she liked it or not, made how small she was sink into her mind. At first glance, Mikoto seemed to act violently and at random, but it was only her understanding all those simple concepts and still looking strange for it. Even street fights had all sorts of manners involved in battles, with the dueling code of honor being a major one. Even now, Shirai knew that Mikoto was way different than she was—all Shirai did was pretend, without really understanding the basics.

She...

Mikoto Misaka...

...would never have made such a blunder. Shirai was sure of it. It was only her opinion as someone selfish, shameless, patronizing, and outside the picture, but she still knew that Railgun wouldn't be in any danger in a crisis like this. She would grin and clash face-first with her opponent, dominating the match without giving them time for a counterattack, then leave without a scratch on her.

She would stand in defiance of such a tiny predicament.

No matter how bad the situation was, she'd never take a single step back.

She would run straight to Shirai. She'd put her, wounds and all, on her back. She'd even throw in a few words of consolation. Then she'd jump out of the building at the very last second.

Maybe she *would* come to the rescue of her idiot underclassman lying here.

Kuroko Shirai thought of Mikoto Misaka's name, and of her face.

And then she smiled a little. *Well, this might be aiming a bit high even for my perfect Big Sister.* Her complacent self-mockery was accompanied by something around her creaking. It sounded almost like a glass pane being pressed on. *Here it comes,* she thought hazily. It didn't look like any teleportation or Move Point she'd seen thus far, but she still knew.

Within the next ten seconds, most likely, 4,520 kilograms of weight would be crossing through space and appear on top of her.

Outside the broken windows, she could hear car engines and the same commotion as before. The gap between that and this room, currently enveloped in an eerie silence—aside from the out-of-place French pop music coming from the speakers, but that was actually giving her the creeps—made her want to smile.

I don't want to die, she thought dimly.

And at the same time, while she knew it would never reach, she prayed as hard as she could to Mikoto Misaka.

To Railgun, who might be rushing here at this very moment, having noticed the commotion.

Please...

Shirai couldn't move at all by herself.

But with someone's support, she could move out of here.

If rescue were to come with this timing...

If someone came for her at the last moment, like one of those old, worn-out superheroes...

Please...

That was what the girl in twin tails wished for.

At the end of it all, one step away from the grand finale, at this very moment.

Just get as...far away from here as you can. Please, do make sure not to get caught in this, Big Sister.

Kuroko Shirai ardently wished for this. She could no longer avoid Awaki Musujime's attack, which would be starting any moment now.

Even if someone came running in for her, the odds of her being saved were slim. If Mikoto were to see this place, she'd probably rush over to the fallen Shirai's side first thing—without a thought to the attack coming through space. Even if her intuition was vivid enough to see the attack coming and she tried to take Shirai out of the building with her, would she even be in time? If worse came to worst, they'd *both* be killed in the building's collapse. Those odds were *not* slim.

But still...

Still...

Ah...

She could hear something.

A banging. Someone's footsteps were climbing up to the entrance to the now-uninhabited floor. Footsteps, running up the emergency stairwell—had they thought using the elevator was too much of a pain?

No, wait, they weren't just footsteps.

Crackle, crackle. With them came the sound of electric sparks flying.

Ahhh...!! No! she thought, her face growing pale.

Her limbs weren't moving, so she couldn't stop those footsteps whether or not she wanted to.

So instead, she moved her mouth. "No...don't! Don't...Please don't come here!" As she spoke, the tears began at how perfect the timing was. She strained her throat, pouring every last bit of stamina into her final shout. "A special attack is coming here! This floor is too dangerous to come to! No, please, get away from the whole building! It's going to collapse!!" she screamed, lying in her own blood on the floor.

The space around her grated and squealed. Was it the herald of Musujime's attack, or was it just a signal? "...?!" *This is bad*, she thought. She had stormed into the restaurant with teleportation, so she didn't know the exact construction and floor plan of the building, but at the very least, she could tell that whoever's footsteps those were, they wouldn't make it to this floor within ten seconds. Going directly here would be one thing, but having to run around all the hallways and staircases like they were would just end up wasting time and distance—it was impossible.

Shirai didn't know in any concrete sense what object Musujime was going to warp in here.

But if 4,520 kilograms of weight all came in at once, it wouldn't just be this floor—the rest of the building would collapse, too. And it would catch anyone inside when it did.

She couldn't allow that.

She absolutely could not allow that.

"Run…away…!!" she tried to shout, on the verge of tears, but she didn't make it. She couldn't make it. A moment later, the air in the room all twisted apart. Her vision suddenly looked like she was seeing the world through a fish-eye lens; it was probably the aftermath of something starting to tear space apart, with the compression rate of air on the floor changing and causing light to refract.

The attack was beginning.

"…!!" Shirai gritted her teeth. She tried as hard as she could.

But her limbs still wouldn't move. Not even a fingertip could move. Her ability wasn't working at all, either. *I hate this*, she thought from the very bottom of her heart. If only she'd been stronger. She could have easily teleported both herself and the person coming to save her right out of the building without a problem. And if she hadn't lost to Awaki Musujime, she would never have been forced into this kind of crisis in the first place.

She didn't have the strength now that she felt that way.

Reality never worked out like that.

Big…Sis…ter…!!

Even through all that, she put the last of her strength into her weakened body. She knew all that would change was how far open her wounds tore needlessly—but she absolutely couldn't allow herself to let go of her energy. And at the same time, she prayed: that some moronic miracle happened and that one single girl, strong but still just a girl, saved her.

Boom!!
Then, as if in answer to her prayers, an orange line stabbed through from the floor to the ceiling.

It was a piece of metal, fired at three times the speed of sound.

The slender heat ray, plunging diagonally through the room like a needle, was going far too fast for the naked eye to observe. It was like a laser, its beginning and end hidden from view. Just a single straight line, burning the air in its wake from its extreme speed.

Shirai, for a moment, looked at it, befuddled.

Then, there was a *thump* as the entire building shook. A storm of destruction sprang forth as though using the orange line as a fuse. An air hole two meters across opened up in the floor, knocking over all the objects right above it, blowing them aside, destroying everything. She felt the floor tilt slightly as she heard the sounds of rubble crashing down to the floors beneath.

Railgun.

The ability and the name of the one who possessed it came to mind, and Shirai, still collapsed in a heap, worked her brain.

"With this much ventilation, there will still be time, right?"

A girl's voice—an all-too-familiar one.

There was no panic, no fear, no doubt in it at all.

It was relaxed, saying the current situation was not even close to a problem.

"I hate to say it, but this is as much as I can do. Now you go and use your fist to bring her back!!"

Shirai was taken aback at the words.

She craned her head, and then she saw.

She saw a person running through the windhole tunnel opened by the Railgun that was stabbing through the concrete floor. She saw a boy running up a staircase of ceiling rubble and furniture from the floor below that had piled up in the diagonally opened windhole leading up to her floor.

He could have never made it with the normal stairs.

So he hadn't used them at all.

There were no weapons in the hands of the boy using such an absurd shortcut. From the looks of it, he didn't have some incredible ability, either. But he still ran. Ran up to this floor, to where there was clearly some abnormal phenomenon occurring. Simply running and clenching his right fist tight as a boulder.

Within a second, the distortion in space would hit its limit and burst from within.

But at that moment, the boy thrust out his fist, without even paying attention to what was flying at him.

Toward the strange thing in front of him—Musujime's attack, so fantastic, so strong, and so unrealistic.

4,520 kilograms of mass.

He swung his fist like a wrecking ball, aiming to crush that enormous weight all at once.

Ker-thump!! The boy's fist collided with the space.

He gritted his teeth, and his fist somehow plunged straight through that space to the other side.

A strange thing happened.

There was suddenly the roar of steel being struck. It was like he was using his fist to flatten out the very distortion in space itself. He was punching away whatever invisible "thing" was disrupting the course of light.

Forced, *direct* interference from a three-dimensional vector into a special eleven-dimensional point. Shirai was always aware of such calculations, so she knew—it was like forcing a one-way road to go in the opposite direction.

As Kuroko Shirai lay there, dazed at the irrationality of it all, the boy said, "Uhh, sorry I'm late. Well, I mean, I sort of ran off without really understanding what was going on. If I hadn't run into Mikoto on the way here, I wouldn't have known what to do—Hey, wait a second! Why are you all busted up like that?!"

The boy ran over in a fluster as though he'd only just noticed the state Shirai was in.

"You...Why...Y-you risked your life for me?" stammered Shirai despite herself. This certainly didn't seem like a person who had successfully pulled off the ridiculous feat of pounding warped space back into its normal shape. So she asked, just to make sure. "I'm a complete stranger, aren't I? You have that kind of power... You may possess such great strength...but how can you be so earnest? How did you get into all this with no hesitation?"

For just a moment, the boy looked taken aback at what she'd said. Then he replied, "I mean, you can ask me why or how, but... to be frank, it's quicker and easier to stand up to things instead of running away, right? Well, I mean, if running away would have saved you, I would have chosen that in a heartbeat."

"It's not...that easy, though! Didn't you feel at all scared or anything?"

The boy didn't seem affected by her words. His response came without a second's hesitation. "Well, I guess I was kinda scared. But hey, I made a promise, right?"

Promise? repeated Shirai in her head as the boy gave a good look around. She wondered what he was doing before realizing an instant later he was checking to see that nobody was around.

Finally, he spoke again in a low, secretive voice. "...Yeah, a promise. To protect Mikoto Misaka and the world around her. With some smug, shy guy whose name I don't even know." He grinned a little. "I was a little late to the party, but I'll ask anyway. Am I holding up my part of that promise right now?"

Shirai gave him a confused look, but finally she got her brain working again and looked around—then stopped on one thing.

Mikoto Misaka, the Railgun, the ace of Tokiwadai Middle School, was running over to them. Running through the giant windhole she'd opened herself. Running to her wound-covered underclassman. Running with a face that looked about ready to cry.

In Kuroko Shirai's eyes was the girl she wanted to protect the most, entirely unharmed.

And thus, she answered, "…Yes, you are doing a fine job of it. Half of it, in any case."

The remaining half was currently fleeing with the luggage using Move Point.

"I see." He must have known something. The boy didn't make any mention of what she'd just said—he simply nodded unflinchingly.

And then he spoke again.

"Then I'll go take care of the other half now."

INTERLUDE FOUR

Awaki Musujime had made it to the edge of Academy City using a safe route.

She had penetration wounds all over her, and she had put on her winter blazer without the sleeve on her naked upper body, but its buttons were a total mess, and she didn't even notice the fact. Her arteries and veins had risen to the surface of her skin from her forced usage of her power, and she was continually spitting out balls of hot breath. She hectically moved her gaze about, without a clue as to what to do or where to begin, muttering to herself under her breath in the meantime. Her face was covered with sweat—nervous sweat, probably. Maybe it was because she'd lost her flashlight, but her power over her ability seemed to be looser now. Her bloody fingers from which her customary flashlight had left were touching the handleless luggage.

An unwanted memory came to mind.

It was essentially an aftereffect of using her ability on her own body. The accident during the curriculum two years ago when it had gone out of control. It had been a simple task—teleport herself into a locked room—but she had made a mistake in the coordinate calculations. When she came out of the teleportation, her foot was inside a wall.

It didn't hurt.

And that's why she didn't particularly hesitate to try and pull her foot inside the wall out of it in one breath. She shouldn't have. For a moment later...

There was a tearing noise.

The sensation of the skin on her foot being shaved away by the jagged cross section of the building material in the wall.

The pain was intense.

Her foot came out of the wall—without its skin attached.

It was like...

It was like a peeled orange...Her soft, elastic, moist flesh and slender blood vessels running atop it like netting...

Guh...grrrghh...!!

She bent over. She was overcome with the urge to vomit from deep in her gut, but she barely managed to hold it back. She could feel her back twitching and trembling. Her feet, moving unsteadily, took the nausea as the signal to stop moving completely.

The nausea had been quelled.

What am...? Now that her feet had stopped, she didn't try to take another step. *What am I...supposed to do...now...?*

Her shattered heart had lost its objective. Her lost mind tried to put it back together—she needed a goal, even if it was temporary. The first thing she saw, of course, was the luggage. She couldn't remember what she wanted to do with it. The only thing racing around in her mind was the means to whatever it was—she had to give this to the outside organization.

*I need...*She took out a small wireless radio. *I need to contact them. Contact...contact. I need to...so I will. Ah-ha-ha...see?...I'm doing what you...you all think is necessary...even now...*

She heard the voice of a familiar client from the other end of the radio. Musujime smiled like a child and started communicating. "This is A001 to M000. After confirming your signal, I will report on the..."

Musujime delivered the instructions that had been given to her in the manual beforehand. But just then, there was a loud burst of static, and she got it away from her body reflexively. After putting it back to her ear, all she could hear were gunshots, bellows, and screams. Growing irritated at the lack of a response, she demanded, "This is A001 to M000. A001 to M000. This is…You can hear me, can't you?! Why won't you answer me?!"

The wireless radio started to creak as she screamed—she'd nearly crushed the thing. There was a man's shriek from the other end. That would have been the voice of the organization's leader.

The gunshots over the radio ceased.

This time, instead of the pathetic man, a woman with a lower voice began to speak.

"Watching from a comfortable seat as you deceive children into working for your own ends, eh? Must be nice. I hold myself to never pointing a weapon at a child, but I won't hesitate to point a weapon at someone *for* a child."

There was a human squeal as a gunshot rang out.

Then the other end of the radio went silent.

"You think I'd just kill you, idiot? Those kids won't be saved until you've coughed up every last bit of information about how many of them you tempted and how you did it."

A moment later, only rough static was coming over the radio. She pushed the button a few times and fiddled with the dial-controlled tuner, but she no longer got any voices. Nobody needed her to contact them.

Ah, ah…I need…I need to contact them…I need to! Why? What do I do? I need a goal, a plan, an objective, or else I'll…!!

Shaking and hitting the radio didn't make it answer, either. Musujime let out a shout, unable to endure the silence, and hurled it to the ground. The delicate parts crashed and scattered across the ground, ending the static. This time, she would really never get an answer, and her face twisted, about to cry.

Musujime didn't have the option available to her of returning to Academy City. For the Academy City General Board chairman, the Tree Diagram wasn't all that important. In fact, if the experiment were restarted, it would cause cracks to appear in the "project" utilizing the ten thousand Sisters. Apparently, that could cause an effect in the power level of the entire *world*, not just within Academy City or in the scientific faction. Musujime, however, didn't understand what such a "world" would mean.

What do I do, what do I do...? For now I should go back to the organization's base...Or maybe I could get in contact with another place instead. Plenty of organizations want what's inside this. Yes, that's right. There're so many things, so many things to do! An objective! As long as I have a goal, I'll be fine!

A twisted smile crossing her face, Musujime, inattentive to the fact that her clothing had been reduced to rags, placed her hands on the luggage. She started walking, pushing it in front of her.

But there was somebody there to stop her from walking.

The *crunch* of a footstep.

There was a single road where she was going. A wide one, surrounded by buildings. Nobody in Academy City was on this path on the outskirts at night—not even a car. The road was like a runway, and somebody was crossing it in front of her.

She didn't think, *Who is it?*

She thought, *They're in the way.* Whoever they were, she'd kill them if they got in her way. Without caution, Musujime marched straight ahead.

Whoever it was, they stopped in the very middle of the six-lane road and blocked her passage.

The shadow of a person...

"The hell?"

...was white with madness, white with crookedness, white with stagnation...

"That dumb brat got some info over the fucking clone network and told me this stuff was related to all those stupid brats. So here I am now, wandering around the city. Seriously, what the hell? They wired up my brain with electricity and even got me a fucking cane to walk with. It's all I had just to get to this dumb place! Choker-shaped electrodes? The only one of its kind in the world? What's *up* with that? That shitty doctor just tossed me some makeshift prototype."

…had electrodes artificially attached to his forehead, temples, and neck, had a tonfa-shaped walking stick with a modern design and handle on his right hand…

"So here I am. And to think I was wondering what kind of delightful *idiot* was responsible for causing me all this pain…So who the *fuck* is this underling?! Are you making fun of me or somethin'?! I didn't need to come all the way out here for this pile of dog shit! At least tell me beforehand it would be some dumb underling! Do you have any idea how much trouble you caused me?!"

Standing in the darkness was Academy City's strongest Level Five.

The pale, pure white Accelerator standing against the blackness, true name unknown.

"Hee…hah…!!"

Just seeing him stopped her breathing and heartbeat for a moment.

H-he's…

A strange burst of air stirred in Awaki Musujime's lungs. She couldn't tell if she was inhaling or exhaling. Her mind was too much of a mess to figure it out.

…It's him!! Why, but, no! Not even Railgun could stand up to him, so there's no way I could…?!

Her mind, spinning its wheels in a fruitless effort to acquire

an objective, suddenly found a much clearer goal even than the luggage—one that could spell her doom.

...I-I-I-I-I have to! I need to do something...!!

She looked at the one blocking her in the middle of the runway-like road and nodded to herself again. She needed to do something. But that was the ultimate question. She needed to do something.

Accelerator was complaining, wondering why Awaki Musujime had to be the one to show up here, but Musujime wanted to take his words and turn them right back at him.

This was more than just a little out of place. This incident was so minor—this feast was nowhere near lavish enough for him to show up for a trivial esper like her. It was like bombing an entire nation just to stop a children's fight.

Musujime's thoughts spun out of control.

This wasn't the same as the skill difference between amateurs and professionals playing sports against one another. It was more like a human playing tug-of-war with a jetliner. You didn't need to explain in detail which one would win. The jetliner didn't have to do anything, and the human wouldn't be able to move a centimeter.

It was over.

It was all over.

Awaki Musujime's face twisted up at the revelation...

But then...

"...I know."

Her face, with distorted muscles, slowly began returning to normal like a ball of string unraveling.

"I know all about it! You don't have your calculation abilities right now. That power you once had is gone! You can't use it! You're not the strongest esper anymore, or even close!!" she shouted as though elated by her triumph.

Accelerator, in the darkness, sighed. "You're pathetic." He

paused, waiting for the wind to blow past. "If you're actually serious, then man, you're so pathetic I almost want to give you a hug."

"Ha-ha! I can see right through your bluff! I was always near that person. I know a little about what's really going on in Academy City. Accelerator, you *lost* your namesake's ability on August thirty-first. Right? If you didn't, then you wouldn't just be standing there! Why don't you attack me? It's not that you won't—you *can't*. You thought you could beat me by using your old title as a shield?"

Her jeering declaration only caused the white one to narrow his eyes.

Musujime took it as him making fun of her, and one of her eyes twitched. "...!! How about you say something?! Don't just stand there; it creeps me the hell out!!" she shouted, while at the same time harboring an odd doubt deep down.

Something was wrong. It was like he didn't match the traits of the Level Five in the data.

"You really are pathetic! Listen up, 'cause I'm only gonna tell you this once." The person spread his arms slowly to either side in the darkness. "I did take some brain damage that day. As you can see by looking at my face, I've gotta outsource all my calculations with these electrodes now. If I go out of range of those damn clones' waves, they can't help me do the calculations. I don't even know if I've got *half* my old power left. I wouldn't last fifteen minutes in real combat with how fucking terrible this thing's battery life is.

"But—" said Accelerator, pausing.

"—just because I've gotten weaker doesn't mean you got any stronger, now, does it?"

His smile appeared to splatter across his face.
He slammed the foot of his crutch into the ground with a *thud!!*
The firm ground shook as though being pressed from under-

neath. Accelerator crouched. Cracks stretched out in the asphalt road, each with him at its origin. The nearby buildings creaked, and all the glass windows, unable to withstand the change in the buildings' structure, shattered, scattering shards of glass everywhere.

No...Impossible...?!

Musujime looked up. The shards were raining down from every building along the main road. She couldn't flee using Move Point. They were covering too wide an area. Fleeing into a building wouldn't be a good plan, either. The windows were broken because the buildings' construction had been distorted. She didn't think the furniture inside was in the same place anymore. In the worst-case scenario, she could finish herself off by using Move Point and jumping right into a collapsed wall.

That means to get away...I need to go up!!

She grabbed the luggage and immediately used Move Point to get herself into the air. She went past the rain of glass and into the night sky dozens of meters above the ground. Simultaneously, she was struck by an overwhelming nausea, but she put all her effort into quelling that. She worked her mind furiously—she wasn't used to this, but she needed to jump again to a different building top before she started to fall...

And then her mind went blank.

The equations she'd been desperately constructing in her mind all blew away.

"Aha-gya-ha! Thank you *very much* for that low-angle shot you're givin' me!!"

Ka-boom!! came an explosion. Accelerator stomped on the broken asphalt again and blasted off into the sky like a rocket. He hadn't only changed the vector of the force his legs exerted. Behind him, there were four powerful, whirlwind-like bursts of air connected to him.

Oddly, to Musujime, it made him look like an angel ascending into heaven.

An angel who had fallen into the pit of the earth, utterly disgraced and defiled, baring his fangs toward Paradise above.

Accelerator tore into the layer of glass rain between them. Then, with a terrible cracking sound, he broke through it all at once. There wasn't a wound left on his body as he launched straight toward Musujime like a bullet.

His fist was already clenched.

He crushed in his grip the walking stick supporting him and it fell away from him like a multistage rocket. The demonic fist came for Awaki Musujime's face with the speed and weight of his whole body behind it.

"...
..........................???!!!"

There was no way for her to remain calm in this situation.

She'd renounced her calculations, and now she abruptly moved the luggage between them to protect herself. Accelerator's fist, however, plunged through her measly defenses, shattering them. The luggage's outer case broke apart, its antishock padding flew away, and the contents, rigidly fixed inside, met their end as a mess of parts and fragments, scattering before Musujime's eyes like a blizzard of cherry blossom petals.

"Sorry, but from here on, it's a one-way road." The corners of the esper's lips turned up. "Meaning you can't come in! So tuck your damn tail between your legs and crawl back to wherever it is you came from!!"

Musujime's throat let out a strange breath of air.

The tightly balled fist, ignoring the mere luggage, collided with her face at a ridiculous speed.

Crunch!!

Awaki Musujime was sent flying even higher up at an angle, high into the sky. She flew toward the edge of a building roof, coming at it from diagonally underneath, then she hit the metal fence meant to prevent people from falling off of it. Several of the fence's braces pulled out of their roots like a forcefully kicked soccer ball breaking through a net. Finally, she came to a stop.

Accelerator, having transferred all his momentum to her, stopped dead in the air. Then, drawn by gravity, he began to fall back down to the dark ground beneath.

He didn't look at the ground.

As he fell, he slowly looked up at the building Musujime had collided with, and said under his breath, "Yeah, if this is all I got, then maybe I've gotta retire the name of Academy City's strongest." Quietly, he closed his eyes. "But still, if it means brats like you don't get to use it, I'll keep on using the title, you fucking trash."

The night wind carried away his unheard words as he fell toward the ground.

EPILOGUE

Their Lives
One_Place, One_Scene.

The next day...

After Touma Kamijou called the school and said he'd be late that morning, he visited a certain hospital. Not for treatment. This time, he really didn't get hurt at all. He was going to visit Kuroko Shirai.

And now he was standing around in a vending-machine-corner-slash-café, a kind of lounge meant for conversation, a little bit away from the hospital room. There was a bright red hand mark on his cheek. When he'd opened the door to visit, Shirai had been changing.

Now that he'd been forcefully expelled from the room, he speculated that she'd probably take a little bit longer to change, so he decided instead to drag the offended Index beside him over to visit Little Misaka's room, which was in the same hospital.

Little Misaka was currently in another room. She had already been undergoing treatment, and yesterday's physical activity had apparently placed her in a good bit of danger. At the moment she was floating in a reinforced glass capsule with clear liquid inside, like from some sci-fi movie, the kind that you would never see at a regular hospital.

She seemed to be conscious inside the capsule, and she bowed to Kamijou expressionlessly when she saw him. However, she was entirely naked save for the electrodes attached to her body with white tape, which caused Index to start chomping on the back of his head on the spot. (Little Misaka didn't care at all.)

And she bit him pretty hard, too—hard enough that the black cat curled up in the pet cage in the corner of the room (specially designed not to let dander or germs outside it) summoned its fight-or-flight instincts. It began raging about, unnaturally scared, as though a huge earthquake were on its way. It was one of those "when it rains, it pours" sort of days.

In any case.

After Kamijou and Index had been chased out of the two hospital rooms, they ended up back in the lounge.

"...What rotten luck. Good old Kamijou is already unlucky on a daily basis, but this is a rotten luck fever (whose chances fluctuate)! Oh, God, if the Nine Gates of bad luck came to me today, I wouldn't be surprised!!"

Beaten up by a couple different people now, Kamijou looked exhausted. He took his bag with the fruit pastry from Kuromitsu House that went for 1,400 yen a pop (while not even being that big) in one hand, as he thought about Index, next to him, possibly just eating the entire bag whole—but now, she would at least have the common sense not to devour a gift for someone at the hospital—still, though, it was worrying.

Index, though, was actually more interested in the lights for the vending machine's lottery roulette than the confectionery. "So I don't know anything about that tree or the rem-whatever, but after you acted all cool and went, *Then I'll go take care of the other half now*, you didn't get anything out of it, did you...?"

"Urk...Well, I went to the route Shirai said she'd run away using. And then I found the entire street corner with all the windows smashed, and wreckage everywhere, and all the contents in a billion pieces, and there was a real roughed-up girl hanging on the roof...I don't know who did it, but I want to thank them for it."

"Touma, Touma. I don't usually use this word, but you're worthless!"

"Hooray, I knew you would say that, damn it!! I want to know who the hell butted in and stole my prey then left without saying anything! How stupid do they need to make themselves look before they're satisfied?!"

"...I think that honestly one of you is enough, Touma."

Another pained shout of *Hooray!* made its way through the morning hospital halls.

"What the hell's goin' on out there? Some idiot tryin' to have a festival in the hallways or what?"

Accelerator scowled at the voices he was hearing from the other side of the wall. The voice sounded somehow familiar, but it was probably just his imagination. The room was for a single person, but it wasn't very big, and Accelerator pulled the covers on the bed in the middle of it back over him. You wouldn't have been able to tell with how strangely long his hair had been growing, how quickly his wounds had been closing, and how high he'd been jumping into the night sky, but he was so wounded any normal person wouldn't have even been able to stand.

There was a table set up across the bed. It was about where a pedestrian walkway would be sitting over a road. It was for eating meals while in bed, but at the moment, there was a girl who looked ten at first glance sprawled out on it, flapping her feet to and fro. Once, she'd been in a terrible state—completely naked save for a blanket—but today she was wearing a children's sky blue camisole. It was one of the articles of clothing the woman in the jersey had brought for her.

"So apparently Yomikawa went *outside* and beat up an organization called the Asociación de Cienia or something, says Misaka says Misaka, announcing the news she got over the network. It seems like Ao Amai had been in contact with them, too, so that's why he knew so much about the Tree Diagram, says Misaka says Misaka with a touch of overflowing realism."

"'Zat so...?"

"So then Yomikawa went home with those shadows under her eyes like she'd been up all night working and stuff, says Misaka says Misaka, calmly remembering that age really can be revealed by how your skin looks and stuff...Wait, you seem waaay less into things than you usually are, you know, says Misaka says Misaka, looking at you sideways."

"...I just got back this morning and I'm sleepy, so can we do this later?"

"Ohhh! I think maybe it would be really bad if you were sleepy, says Misaka says Misaka, transforming into alarm clock Misaka! Come on, it's morning, and it'll be afternoon in two hours, says Misaka says Misaka, flapping her feet around and encouraging you to wake the heck up before your sleepiness gets the better of you like some spoiled brat!!"

"..."

Did she have some experience where my sleeping did something bad to her or something? Accelerator, dubious, pulled the covers over him and plugged his ears. He could employ his power to a certain extent by using the electrodes and having the Misaka Network do it, but that normally didn't get allotted to any more than general speech and calculation functions and the absolute minimum reflection needed, such as for ultraviolet rays. Otherwise it would just drain the prototype's battery.

"You must really have it nice, you stupid brat. I nearly died getting out of this hospital with my brain like a milkshake, and I did all that work until this morning cleaning up afterward, and meanwhile you're snoring away in bed with your damn air conditioner somehow getting results—guh, urgh. I implore you not to take away my language processing capabilities based on reasons originating in religious beliefs, please!!" shouted Accelerator angrily, his words losing their normal shape midway through.

The Misaka Network had suspended its proxy calculations for Accelerator's speech center.

In other words, he was trying to say, "Don't take away my ability to talk just because it's convenient for you."

"Misaka doesn't do your proxy calculations for you to hurl abusive language at her, retorts Misaka retorts Misaka cutely—wait, *bfft!* Why are you wrapping Misaka up in that blanket, asks Misaka asks Misaka, sensing a little bit of danger!!"

Meanwhile, in the room next door…

"N-n-n-n-n-now, n-n-n-now, Big Sister. It is finally time for the moment of supreme bliss where you feed me, Kuroko Shirai, apple slices cut into little bunny rabbits! Heh-heh, heh-heh-heh-heh-heh!!"

"Be quiet, shut up, how are you this freaking energetic after what happened yesterday, Kuroko?! —Wait, you don't actually have the energy?! If you're forcing yourself to crawl across the bed like that with sheer willpower, you're really gonna kill yourself!!"

Kuroko Shirai, massively wounded, grinned happily and tried to get closer to her "big sister," but Mikoto Misaka managed to push her back into bed and tuck her in.

"Ah, ahh…This sensation, of Big Sister's hands violently shoving me into bed…I-I suppose I really was correct for getting involved in that life-threatening melee combat. The world—the whole world is shining so brightly right now!"

"Do you not understand what the doctors told you?! Complete, quiet bed rest!!"

"If you want me to settle down, then please, feed me those bunny apple slices. Come to think of it, wouldn't that gentleman who came in here before prefer a more family-oriented girl?"

"...R-really? I mean...Hey, Kuroko, do you really think so?"

"There you go reacting so innocently to something I totally said at random, Big Sister! I knew it! I knew it—it was that jerk who came in the room while I was changing!! You were with him!! That little punk!!"

Mikoto stood dumbfounded at Shirai's wondrous vitality. *How is she thrashing about so vigorously when she's so badly hurt, anyway?* It was enough to make her almost forget why she'd come to visit her in the first place. And she felt a pang of regret at not giving the certain young man who walked in on them a firm palm strike (with a moderate *biri biri* attached) in place of Shirai, who couldn't move like she wanted to with her injuries. The after-incident report she'd gotten of Awaki Musujime being treated as a study-abroad student at her own school, Kirigaoka Girls' Academy, didn't seem at all important to her anymore.

The conversation's rhythm came to an abrupt halt.

There was a short silence.

The warm air in the room started to cool down.

It took more strength than she thought it would to reopen the closed window.

Mikoto knew exactly why.

There were several stab wounds on her underclassman's body.

After all was said and done, she'd gotten *another* person mixed up in this.

First the Sisters, then that boy, and now her simple underclassman.

"You know, I...," began Shirai from the bed, interrupting her thoughts. Mikoto gave her a slightly confused look, and Shirai smiled. "I suppose that I realize it now. The place you were that night—it was the world you're fighting in. Nothing about it made the least bit of sense to me. And after you came running up to me at the end, I stopped thinking a few times, as absurd as that sounds." She laughed just a little bit and loosened slightly. "I don't think I can stand there as I am now. I forced myself into that world once, and this is how it turned out."

"Kuroko..." Mikoto's expression betrayed her pain at the thought—but a new one immediately hid it. She was the sort to hide that kind of feeling. Shirai knew that was exactly the reason Mikoto was so fragile, though.

"Big Sister, if you are thinking that it is your fault for getting me mixed up in this incident, I'm afraid you are entirely mistaken."

"Huh?"

"What did you expect? My weakness is my own fault. What do you have to do with that, Big Sister? I would much rather you not make fun of me. I am able to carry out my own responsibilities by myself. Making you shoulder those burdens rips my pride to pieces," she said dully. "I would much rather you smile, Big Sister. Your underclassman failed but still returned safely—you should be laughing uproariously at me, pointing and asking me how I screwed up so badly. With that sort of amusing memory to nourish me, I would be able to stand back up again."

And one more thing, she added to herself. *This only goes for me as I am now. Not a hair on Kuroko Shirai's head wishes to stop where she is. I will not make you wait long, Big Sister. When Kuroko has a destination in mind, she gets there fast.*

Now that she knew how good it felt here, she could resolve herself to return from any battlefield.

Quietly, so that the girl at her side would never know.

This was how Kuroko Shirai learned where she stood.

And how she realized there was a world her hands couldn't reach.

However, that was why she wouldn't give up—she would reach her hands higher and higher.

But not at all because she wanted to feel that she was above anyone.

Only because she wanted to protect the one place she was in right now.

AFTERWORD

Hello again to those of you reading one volume at a time.

Nice to meet you, those of you who bought all eight volumes in the set.

I'm Kazuma Kamachi.

On to the eighth volume! The theme this time was supernatural abilities, once and for all. In a curveball from other volumes, the only actual male character to appear is Touma Kamijou. For those of you suspicious of that, I'd ask you to defer your judgment for now. It's nothing to be dealt with lightly.

This volume picks up on a few of the unsolved problems from volumes 3 and 5. It may have seemed at first to be unrelated to anything occult, but I think that the villain Awaki Musujime's doubts had some occult factors in them.

Why was there a difference in power between Mikoto Misaka and Little Misaka? Could other animals or plants measure and analyze phenomena and drive their own abilities? Just what *is* phenomenon measurement and analysis, anyway? These questions weren't answered in this volume because of how the story is put together and the viewpoint of the main character, but that means we can leave the mystery to stew.

*   *   *

I'd like to give an immense thank-you to my illustrator, Mr. Haimura, and my editor, Mr. Miki. It's thanks to the two of you that this book safely made its way to store bookshelves.

And I'd like to give an unconditional thank-you to everyone who purchased this book. It's thanks to you that this book safely made its way to *your* bookshelves.

Now then, as I give thanks for the fact that this book is now somewhere in the corner of your mind,

and as I consider it an honor if you could continue to put future volumes back there as well,

today, at this hour, I lay down my pen.

...Mikoto Misaka. She was supposed to be in this a whole lot more...

Kazuma Kamachi